Star Struck

Janet —

I hope you laugh

Star Struck

by
Josi S. Kilpack

BONNEVILLE BOOKS
Springville, Utah

ISBN: 1-55517-792-1
e.2

Published by Bonneville Books
Imprint of Cedar Fort Inc.
www.cedarfort.com

Distributed by:

Cover design by Nicole Shaffer
Cover design © 2004 by Lyle Mortimer

Printed in the United States of America
10 9 8 7 6 5 4 3 2 1
Printed on acid-free paper

Library of Congress Control Number: 2004096570

Dedication

To my girls:
Lindsy, Breanna, Madison & Kylee—
May your internal Delilah so shine!

Authors Notes

No animals were injured in the production of this book—
not even the chickens. All events are fictional; any similarity to
actual events is purely coincidental . . . and downright creepy.

Acknowledgments

There are always so many people to put on this page—words are not enough to express the deep appreciation I feel. Thank you to the reader to whom I owe so much; this book wouldn't be here if people didn't want a good read. Your ongoing support and enthusiasm is priceless to me and keeps me writing on days the words won't come.

Specifically let me thank my mom for giving me the love of reading and my dad for the example that talents are meant to be developed. Thanks to the friends and family members that keep encouraging me and asking when the next one comes out. Big hugs to my kids for being patient with my writing and enjoying the ride with me. Thanks to my manuscript readers, my dear sister Crystal White, and my friend Tristi Pinkston (author of *Nothing to Regret* www.tristipinkston.com). Thanks to Annette Lyon (*At the Waters Edge* www.annettelyon.com)for her help with content and BJ Rowley (*Light Traveler* series www.bjrowley.com) for his wonderful editing skills. Duke Hollingshead (Mr. H) double checked my dairy farm information—thank you thank you for making sure I made sense. Big thanks to the members of LDStorymakers for their continual support and friendship and to CFI for believing in me yet again.

Thanks too big for words for my sweetie and best friend Lee, who makes everything in my life possible and gives me so many reasons to smile. Last but certainly not least, to my Father in Heaven for all of the above and so much more. I'm a very lucky girl, thanks everybody.

✯ Chapter One ✯

The makeup girl hurried to finish with the powder on Samuel Hendrick's face while he tapped his fingers and waited as patiently as he could, pretending not to notice the coy glances she'd been giving him for the last ten minutes. Normally, Sam would have enjoyed a little flirtation, but his thoughts weren't concentrated on women—a rare event for the hottest actor of the new century. On one hand, Sam couldn't believe he was finally getting an interview with Trisha P, the newswoman-turned-interviewer and host of the popular evening news show *One on One with Trisha P*. The P was short for Pompiskoloski, or something similarly impossible to pronounce. For obvious reasons, she'd always gone by Trisha P. On the other hand, he couldn't understand why he hadn't been featured on her show sooner. He was Sam Hendricks after all. But he couldn't find much to complain about. This chair on this night was the most coveted seat in Hollywood, and it was all his. Tonight's show, the night of Oscar nominations, would be watched almost as closely as the actual award ceremony eight weeks from now . . . and Sam was the one warming the cushions.

Behind him, positioned so that it would fit in view of the camera, was a poster of his latest movie, *Samson and Delilah*. It was the fourth year in a row that he'd been nominated for an Oscar, but he'd failed to go home with the golden man clutched in his fist each of the three preceding years. This was his year though, he could feel it. For the first time he'd been nominated for a leading role rather than a supporting one, and everyone was saying that he was a shoo-in. When he'd been asked to do the movie over three years ago he hadn't been sure it would be that popular. It was a Bible story, after all. But the script was tight and the actress playing Delilah was hot. It also offered him a leading role—something that had eluded him to that point. *Samson and Delilah* had been released at the end of the year, just in time to make it into this year's Academy Award nominations. It had been the best-selling box office production for seven weeks running and was still going strong. So far, it had grossed nearly four hundred million dollars. His cut was only sixteen million, and it irritated him that he hadn't held out for more. However, if he won the Oscar, he'd never again complain about being ripped off.

A hush fell over the set, and he looked to his left as Trisha P walked onto the stage. She was reading a stack of notes and had apparently had her hair and makeup done in her dressing room. The paper bib placed around Sam's neck to keep his Armani shirt makeup free, was removed. He tried to look casual as Trisha approached, seemingly oblivious to everything going on around her. She sat in the red velvet chair across from him and continued scanning her notes as Sam shifted his position, trying to find one that would be comfortable yet look attractive to the estimated 60 million viewers of the show.

"Stop fidgeting," Trisha said without looking up. "The cameras are already rolling, and you'll make the director nervous if you keep squirming around like that."

Sam stopped fidgeting.

After what seemed like hours she raised her hand and snapped her fingers. Within seconds her hair got a final pat, the hem of her skirt was pulled down to her knees, and the notes were removed from sight. She looked up at Sam with her deep blue eyes and smiled as if she'd known him all her life, which wasn't far from the truth. They had met at least a dozen times at various parties or premieres, and she was friends with both of his Hollywood parents. However, this was the first time he'd ever been interviewed on her show.

"Don't be nervous, Sam," she said in a motherly tone.

"I'm not nervous," he said with a smile. It was a lie—but what good was it to be an actor if you couldn't lie now and then?

"Good," she said with a nod. Then she looked toward the camera and indicated that she was ready. It took another minute or two for the final adjustments to be made, but finally the director began counting down from twenty. Instead of saying "One" he yelled, "Roll it."

The interview began.

Trisha welcomed the viewers and then turned to face Sam. "I do believe this is the first time you and I have ever done a sit-down interview, Sam—or should I call you Sam-son."

Sam laughed and shook his head as if to say "Oh, Trisha." "Sam is fine," he said instead. He tilted his head to the side and grinned his famous half-smile. Across America, he imagined women of all ages swooning, men sucking in their bellies, and everyone wanting to either be him or be with him. There was no doubt in his mind that it was more than just his imagination. Everyone loved him—they'd all said so.

"There is a certain parallel though, isn't there?" Trisha continued. "Samson was promised that so long as he didn't cut his hair he'd retain his incredible strength, and I believe you haven't cut your own hair for several years. It's become your trademark—and you seem to have fulfilled the superstition with the incredible success of this movie."

"Well, it didn't happen for me quite like it did for Samson. I made the promise to myself not to cut my hair when I finished that last round of drug rehab." He paused to put the words in the proper order he and Cody, his personal assistant, had practiced. He wanted to make sure he said everything just right. "I learned in rehab just how important it was for me to claim my own identity and to break away from the roles I'd been forced into. Not cutting my hair has become a physical symbol of my independence—my manhood, you could say." He winked at the camera. "Every morning I'm reminded of who I really am by simply seeing that reflection in the mirror. When this movie came up, I just happened to be the only actor with the right length of hair for the role of Samson."

They could have easily chosen whoever they wanted and had the perfect wig made, but they hadn't, and he'd continually joked that his hair was the only feature that had landed him the role. The American public often said his humility was his third most endearing trait. The first was his rugged good looks and the second was his chiseled physique.

"This is your fourth Oscar nomination in four years. It's an impressive tribute to your own strength in this business," Trisha continued.

"I've just been lucky so far," Sam said with more of that adorable humility.

"But do you think this year is your year? Will you go home with the Oscar this time?"

"I'm sitting with you, aren't I?"

The actors that had won Best Actor for the last five years had sat where he was sitting now. It was a very good sign.

The next fifteen minutes were spent recapping the events of his life that had brought him here. They touched on his years playing minor child roles in his dad's movies, to getting a spot on the popular sitcom "Life with Ronny Coop" that ran until he was fourteen years old. After that he'd played some small parts here and there, but at sixteen was sent to rehab for the first time. At eighteen he was sent again, and at nineteen he escaped jail time for assault and battery by going to rehab again. The third time had been the charm, and he'd been clean ever since—if you didn't count beer with whisky chasers.

When he came back to show biz after the final stint with Betty Ford, he'd decided to be totally candid and open about his past. He had hoped it would cast him in a more favorable and sympathetic light. It had worked. The great public tribunal loved it. He started playing secondary characters in big movies immediately, sometimes doing two movies a year. Until this past year he really wasn't old enough, nor had he had enough movie experience, to land him the leading roles, but he'd done well for himself and now he would always be known as the one and only Samson.

The role of Samson had launched him into a league of actors with the likes of Tom Cruise, Sean Connery, and Russell Crowe. In fact, rather than do another movie right after, as he had always done before, he had decided to wait—really whet the appetite of his fans and hold out for another major role. It meant he wouldn't have a movie out in time for next year's

Oscars, but since he was sure he'd go home with the golden statue this year, he felt alright about it. There were three scripts currently waiting for his evaluation. All of them were leading roles. He was moving up.

Trisha continued to move the interview along. "This brings us back to the Oscar, for which you've been nominated . . . again."

Sam smiled and nodded. "Who'd have thought," he said.

Trisha P laughed. "And that leads us to the big question all of America is asking: who will be your date?"

At the time of his first nomination, Sam had been nineteen years old and involved with Kanisha Pane, a world-renowned supermodel. Things hadn't been going well between them. Their involvement had been fuel for both careers, and when he learned she'd been touring Europe with one of the Backstreet Boys he ended the farce. After weeks of pressure concerning who would attend the Oscars with him, now that Kanisha wasn't an option, Sam asked the fifty-five-year-old nanny who had practically raised him. Kanisha's rejection was a bitter blow, and he hadn't wanted to pretend he wasn't heartbroken by showing up with a new love interest. What he hadn't expected, however, was the public's reaction to his date. The American celebrity watchers loved the idea of him taking someone like them to the most touted event of the year. Overnight, his image went from betrayed lover to Robin Hood.

He'd had the good sense to make the most of their reaction. By sending the nanny on a one hundred thousand dollar shopping spree and inviting her to spend a week at the best resort in Miami Beach to rest up for the big event, he turned a simple decision into an extraordinary event. On the big day, she received a celebrity makeover and arrived on his arm looking like a diva in a Ralph Lauren gown made especially for her. The experience made the cover of *People Magazine*, and the nanny landed a role in a movie not long afterward.

The following year he decided to play up the "peasant date for the Oscars." This time, he asked the woman doing his makeup right before an interview on Jay Leno following his nomination. She'd nearly passed out with surprise, but of course she'd accepted. The news was announced that night on Leno, and the following week the makeup artist's transformation began. This makeover was a bit harder than the nanny's since this girl weighed in at 260 pounds. After a month at a health spa and another Hollywood make over, she captured the hearts of America when she stepped out of the limo looking like a million bucks—which wasn't too far off what it had cost to get her down to a size fourteen. These days she was back doing makeup for Jay, but she'd enjoyed months on the talk-showcircuit and had recently become the spokeswoman for Jenny Craig.

Last year had been even trickier. It was expected that he would do it a third time, so he held off all the questions for nearly a month. He didn't ask anyone until one week before the show. The lucky girl was his dental hygienist. She was 30 years old and cute as a button. A week later, she was transformed into a Hollywood vixen and had recently been featured on Saturday Night Live along with her boyfriend, Tommy Lee.

In three years, three women's lives had changed dramatically because of one night spent on his arm. It was a tribute to how powerful he really was.

Ever since this year's nominations had been announced—a whole ten hours ago—he'd had women falling over themselves to get noticed.

"So, who's the lucky lady going to be this year?" Trisha asked.

He shrugged. "I don't know yet."

"Are you going to wait till a week before the award ceremony, like last time?"

"I'm not really sure." He leaned forward slightly. "But I'll make you a promise, Trisha," he said. Most of the interview had been scripted. He'd received the questions weeks ago and had rehearsed his answers. But this was a twist all his own.

Trisha raised an eyebrow.

"If you'll keep a camera ready to go, I'll let you be there."

Even for a woman as seasoned and refined as Trisha P, this

was an intriguing venture. He saw the glimmer of excitement in her eyes. A slow smile spread across her face and she nodded. "You're on."

✲ Chapter Two ✲

"You can't keep the world waiting forever," said Cody Jenkes, Sam's personal assistant, as they drove down 31st street in Manhattan. It had been nearly a week since his appearance on *One on One with Trisha P* had aired. He still hadn't asked a date, and attention from the press was getting worse every day. He'd flown from his beach house in Malibu to his apartment in New York in hopes of escaping. It hadn't worked.

He'd been all but shut in his New York apartment since his arrival, due to paparazzi, press reporters, and miscellaneous women waiting to catch a glimpse of him. A woman that had fitted him for a new suit two weeks ago claimed that he'd asked her to be his date; of course he hadn't. Other rumors were surfacing as well, but the only thing he'd said to the press was that he certainly hadn't asked anyone yet. When he did, the whole world would know about it. That just made the press drool even more.

Sam was used to attention and didn't mind being in the spotlight, but this was getting ridiculous. This morning, Cody had insisted they get out of the apartment and go to lunch. In order to get out undetected, Sam traded clothes with one of his bodyguards. The press had grown accustomed to the other man's comings and goings, so it was relatively easy to slip by them. Now, he was in the back of his Bentley, heading for a small café in Greenwich Village where Cody assured them total privacy.

"How much longer do you think you can stand this?" Cody continued.

"About an hour," Sam said as he ran his fingers through his long dark hair, grimacing at the rumples it had incurred while being shoved under the ball-cap disguise. Once it was combed out, it hung a few inches past his shoulder, but if he wasn't being filmed, he preferred to pull it back into a ponytail at the base of his neck. It really was an obnoxious trademark. He blew out a breath as New York's Lower East Side crept slowly by on the other side of the tinted window. The traffic was horrible. "I'm going to ask the lucky girl today—after lunch."

Cody did a double take. "You sound like you have someone in mind."

Sam shrugged. There wasn't much about his life that he planned and executed himself; Cody took care of most everything. But now and then it was fun to surprise him. Sam liked to think it kept Cody on his toes. "I don't have a specific girl in mind," Sam continued, "but I know how I'm going to find her. I can't stand this anymore. If I get it over with, she'll take most of the attention off me, and I can get back to living my life."

"So what's the plan? You seem to have it all worked out."

"I do," Sam said with a cocky smile. "After lunch we're going to Central Park, to that statue of Hans Christian Anderson. It's poetic, really. I'll find some ugly duckling and make her into my very own swan."

"What about Trisha P? You promised her footage."

"Go ahead and put her on alert. She said she'd have a New York crew on standby. I'll give them the final details when we finish lunch; they can meet us there."

"The place is going to be crazy," Cody said as he pulled his cell phone out of his jacket pocket. "I'd better call in some extra security to meet us at the park."

"Good idea," Sam said with a smile as he looked back out the window. It would be nice to get this over and done with.

An hour and a half later, seven men tried not to draw attention to themselves as they waited for the lucky girl to arrive on the scene. Trisha P was at her LA studio and unable to come, of course. The camera man she'd arranged for stood close to some bushes so that no one noticed the monstrous equipment he was waiting to use. It was cold enough that the park patrons didn't pay much attention anyway as they hurried by. Several women had come to see the statue or pond that was on the opposite side of the walkway, and each time a woman came into view, everyone involved would look at Sam. Each time Sam shook his head. It was going on twenty minutes when Cody walked over to where Sam was standing near the statue.

"How long are we going to judge this beauty contest before we crown a winner?" he asked, shifting from one foot to the other.

"I want just the right girl this year. Someone the world can relate to."

"What do you mean? Ten women just like that have passed by already."

Sam shook his head. "I don't want a mother," he said. "And I don't want an old lady. I want the kind of woman who watches my movies, who is ordinary and average—but young. A girl I can transform. Just calm down. I'll know her when I see her."

Cody let out a sigh of frustration and walked away, muttering under his breath. Sam didn't care. He turned his head and continued his search for the lucky girl.

★★★

Delilah pulled the collar of her coat up to better shield her neck from the frigid air. She wished she'd brought the scarf her mom had knitted her for Christmas. It was made of the softest yarn she'd ever touched and rivaled anything she'd ever seen at the flashy New York boutiques. But it was at the Jensen's house in the coat closet, and she was in Central Park, freezing to death. She wrapped her gloved hand tighter around Jason's and looked down at him with a smile. Since coming to New York nine months ago, she'd found a hundred things she hated about the city, but there were two things she'd grown to love very much. One was the little boy she cared for as a nanny. Jason was five years old, the only child of very successful and, therefore, very busy parents. He was bright and well-mannered with light blond hair and bright eyes that brimmed with excitement.

Her other love was Central Park, and lucky for her, Jason loved it too. The two of them escaped the cramped brownstone to come here almost every day, and she still doubted she'd seen the whole thing. The noise and pollution in this city drove her crazy—it was so totally opposite the quiet farm life she'd come from. But Central Park made it all bearable. It was usually while walking along one of the meandering paths that she would determine that she could handle the city for another twenty-four hours. The next day she would come back, fed up with the noise and grayness again, and have the same calming experience. She'd lived one day at a time for nine months. She had three months to go before her one year contract ended. Then she would leave New York forever, marry her high-school sweetheart, and live happily ever after in her hometown of Big Fork, Utah.

Contrary to the name, there was nothing big about Big Fork. Its population of 1,600 was smaller than some of New York's elementary school enrollments. And that's the way she liked it. If she'd ever thought Big Fork was confining and lacked opportunity, New York had convinced her otherwise. She missed open spaces, sunshine, and the friendliness of southern Utah—she couldn't wait to get back.

Today, she and Jason had gone to the Metropolitan Museum and were headed toward the statue of Hans Christian Anderson, one of her favorite areas of the park. It was located in the northeast section, and they often began or ended their outings with a visit to the huge bronze statue of a man seated on a stone bench with a book in his lap. It reminded her of her grandfather and the way she snuggled in his lap when she was a little girl. The sky was gray today, which wasn't saying much since it was always gray, but it was colder than usual. There were still plenty of die-hards, like her, enjoying the park despite the near numbing temperatures.

As they approached the statue, Jason let go of her hand and ran ahead. "Come on, Delilah," he shouted over his shoulder.

"I'm coming," she hollered back.

She shoved her hands in her pocket and wiggled her nose to see if it would still move—she'd lost feeling in it several minutes ago. Her thick blonde hair, topped with a black knit cap, kept her head warm, thank goodness. And she was glad she had always worn her hair long. She needed all the insulation she could get today.

She watched Jason jump up on the platform. He immediately patted the bronze knee, and Delilah smiled. As she caught up with him, she noticed his shoe had become untied. She bent down and retied the laces. When she stood, he ran off to jump onto the short wall that bordered the back portion of the alcove. At that same moment she noticed a man in dark clothes and sunglasses heading toward her from the pond side of the path.

She thought she might have passed him on the walkway, but she couldn't be sure. The hood of his black sweatshirt was up over his head, making it difficult to see the features of his face. Her heart skipped a beat as fear rose in her chest. She was used to small towns, where you didn't just know everyone in town by name, but you knew their kids, their parents, and their pets. New York wasn't like that, and she was never sure what to expect when someone approached her.

In an attempt to get out of his way, she hurried to Jason and stayed close as he pretended that the low wall was a balance beam. A few seconds passed, and she glanced over her shoulder to see if the man in black was still around. He was only a few feet away, and she swallowed as she turned back and said a little prayer that he would leave her alone. He was probably a transient wanting money. All she had was cab fare home, and she had brief visions of being shot in the head for not handing over a quarter. Then again, she was in a public place, one of the safest areas in the park, in fact. Surely, she'd be fine.

"Hi," the man in black said a few seconds later.

She looked at him quickly, noting that he had removed his sunglasses. His face was clean shaven, with a strong jaw, snapping brown eyes, and beautiful teeth. He was also wearing a brand-name sweatshirt that looked new. He didn't look like a transient, but she didn't feel much relief. Why was he singling her out? After another quick glance, she thought he looked somewhat familiar. "Hi," she said in a soft voice and then busied herself with adjusting the hat on Jason's coat.

"Are you enjoying the park today?"

I was, she thought to herself. "Sure," she said, giving him a polite smile. He smiled back, as if he knew something she didn't. It made her even more uncomfortable. She then noticed several other people that seemed to be closing in on the two of them. One of them held a large camera. She looked around frantically before looking back at the man who had addressed her. "What's going on?" she asked apprehensively.

As if to answer the question, he pulled back the hood of his sweatshirt. He said nothing, just smiled at her again as if words weren't necessary. Long brown hair disappeared at the point where his broad shoulders met his tanned neck. His hair seemed to shine despite the lack of sunlight—but she still couldn't place that face, although she felt certain she should know him.

She stared at him for a moment, and then the camera and entourage made sense—sort of. He was someone famous, but she couldn't remember his name, and she hated that she'd been pulled into this, whatever it was.

"Are you Johnny Depp?" she asked as she mentally searched for a name to attach to this face she knew she'd seen somewhere.

His smile faltered, and he seemed unsure of how to respond for half a second, then he quickly repaired his expression. "No," he finally said, trying to laugh, although it seemed forced. "I'm wondering what you're doing on March seventh."

She blinked and tried to make sense of what he'd just said. "What?" she asked again. Jason had stopped his game to watch the show, and she pulled him close, although he remained on the wall.

"March seventh is the night of this year's Academy Awards. I'd like you to go with me."

She continued racking her brain, trying to remember who he was. She was so confused. "You don't even know me," she said after a long silence. She looked around at the camera and the group of people watching with rapt attention. The fear and confusion began to transition into annoyance, which she knew would soon be anger. Apparently, she'd been selected for some stupid Hollywood game. She was not amused.

"We'll get to know each other," he said with that silly plastic grin firmly planted on his face. Then full recognition dawned. This was that Hendricks actor-guy—she didn't have a clue what his first name was. She knew he was in movies, but they were all rated R and so she hadn't seen them. He grinned at her, and she felt the anger rise again. It really didn't matter who he was or what he wanted—she wasn't interested.

"Thanks, but I don't think so." She pulled Jason off the low wall, took his hand, and started to walk away. She just wanted to get away from here—nothing more. Then she could try to make sense of what had just happened.

The man grabbed her arm. "What?"

"I mean, thanks, I'm flattered, really. But that's not my thing. Thanks, anyway."

"It's the Oscars."

"I'm not into it," she said with another polite smile as she pulled her arm away again. She managed two steps before he was suddenly standing in front of her. His face had been put back together with his plastic smile in place once more, and her irritation continued to grow.

He was laughing as if she were playing some joke on him. "I'll give you a call, and we'll work out the details. Now for the record, I know you're first name is Delilah, but what's your last name? I really should know your full name if we're going to go to the Oscars together." He looked at the camera and grinned. All those gleaming smiles aimed at the camera made her wonder if they weren't shooting a toothpaste commercial.

It took a full two seconds for Delilah to get over her surprise at his blatant disregard of her answer. She'd always been headstrong and independent, and she'd never been the kind of girl that didn't get heard. When she spoke now, she made sure to speak loud and clear, enunciating every word just as she would for a small child. She wanted there to be no confusion of what she was about to say, not for him, for the camera, or the growing crowd. "I said I don't want to go with you, Mr. Hendricks. I'm not interested. What part of that have I not made clear? Because I have no problem repeating myself if you find yourself unable to make sense of my answer—it's no . . . thank you."

Everyone around them froze as if captured in a photograph. Delilah took the opportunity to pick Jason up and run. Within ten steps she had half a dozen people following her, but they seemed hesitant, as if unsure of what they were going to do if they caught up. On the other hand, she knew exactly what she was doing—getting out of there—as quickly as possible. Moving as fast as she could, she held Jason close and sighed with relief when Fifth Avenue came into view. Her chest was burning, and she didn't know how much longer she could carry him. The people following her were speeding up. She hadn't a clue how this had happened, why she'd been chosen, but she hated it and wanted to get as far away from it as she could. Jason started to cry and she shushed him as she tried to wave down a cab. Two taxis passed before one pulled to the curb. Just in time. The followers had about caught up. She dove into the taxi, pulled the door shut, and locked it.

"Twenty-Fourth Street," she said breathlessly as hands began to slap against the windows trying to stop the car. She flinched and moved toward the center of the back seat, pulling Jason closer to her chest. The cab-slapping crowd immediately began to flag down cabs of their own. She sank farther down into the seat and told the driver to hurry.

Two hours later, Delilah was on the verge of tears—something that didn't happen often. Within an hour of returning to the Jensen's brownstone apartment, the story was on TV. Her refusal of Sam Hendrick's invitation was a major story. As she watched the segment on a magazine show, she sank lower and lower into her chair. The whole thing was still a blur, and she wasn't sure what had happened to her peaceful stroll in Central Park. Maybe she had acted rashly. Perhaps she should have accepted. But she didn't *want* to go to the Oscars with some celebrity. Yuck. She was Delilah Glenshaw from Big Fork, Utah. The Oscars were a different world for different people. This wasn't her life. How and why did it happen to her, anyway? At least they didn't know who she was.

Someone knocked at the door, and she answered it without thinking. A microphone was thrust into her face, and a man asked her if she'd really turned down Sam Hendricks. A camera was pointed at her face. She slammed the door and felt her lip start to tremble. Then the phone rang; maybe it was one of the Jensens. It wasn't. It was a reporter from some newspaper who wanted to do an exclusive. This was insane. *How did they find me?* she wondered. *How do they know who I am?* She slammed down the phone and began to panic. Regardless of how badly she wanted this to never have happened, it wasn't going away. The phone rang again, and she didn't dare answer it.

The Disney movie she'd put in downstairs ended, and Jason came upstairs bursting with energy just as the doorbell rang. Delilah was still trying to decide whether or not to answer the phone when she heard Jason pull the front door open. She spun around and said the words that were about to define the next four days of her life. "Don't answer that!"

⭐ Chapter Three ⭐

"I just can't believe she said no," Cody said for the hundredth time. It was rare that Cody didn't know how to handle a situation, and his lack of ideas made Sam even more anxious. They'd been back at Sam's apartment trying to formulate a plan for nearly half an hour and they had come up with nothing. The shock had yet to fully wear off.

Sam shook his head. "I shouldn't have asked some stranger. I should have played it like I did last year and waited to see the stars in her eyes. I heard that boy call her 'Delilah' and didn't think it through. Why did you let me do this!" He clenched his jaw and muttered under his breath, "Johnny Depp." He started pacing back and forth in front of his couch.

"It was your idea!" Cody countered. He took a breath as if to calm himself. "Okay, so what do you want to do now?"

"I don't know!" Sam said as he spun around. "How should I know! Why don't you come up with something this time! You're my business manager, my assistant—the man responsible for everything I do and say. Start assisting. Think of something!"

The phone rang, and Cody answered it as Sam continued to pace, shaking his head as he replayed the event in his mind. Cody hung up several seconds later and turned to face Sam.

"Well, I got her name—Delilah Glenshaw. She's a nanny for a family here in the city. I got the address and phone number."

"Call her," Sam ordered.

Cody nodded and picked up the phone to dial the number. He shook his head and hung up a short time later. "She didn't answer."

"Then let's go find her."

Thirty minutes later the car turned the corner and slowed down due to the unprecedented congestion of traffic. The brownstone that bore the correct address was under media

siege. Sam's heart sank, and he told the driver to get them out
of there. Why hadn't he waited to ask someone once he got
back to California? East coast people were obstinate and cold.
He should have known better. As they passed in front of the
house, some reporter did a double take of the car, figured out
who they were, and led the way. Before Sam knew it, there were
reporters everywhere—on the hood, pounding the windows. It
took another forty minutes for them to get back home and less
than a minute to find the story of him driving by her house. He
turned off the TV and kicked his ottoman across the room,
cringing at the pain in his foot that accompanied the dramatic
display. *Great*, he thought to himself as he hopped around on
one foot. *Just great!*

"I'm so sorry," Mrs. Jensen said tenderly, with a hand on
Delilah's arm. "But we just can't keep living like this."

Delilah swallowed the lump in her throat and smiled. "I
understand, really." And she did understand. For the last four
days the apartment had been like a battleground. Her refusal to
talk to the press had made it all the more interesting to the
media, and the family had been hounded day and night. It was
hard to fault the Jensens for letting her go. Their lives had been
turned upside down. But it was still painful to be let go for
something that was no fault of her own.

Mrs. Jensen continued, "Mr. Jensen has come up with a plan
to get you to the airport. He's rented four cars that look the
same. We have three women from his office coming, and all of
you will take one bag and wear a brown coat with a hood. You'll
each go in different cars and drive off in different directions.
Mr. Jensen and I will explain to the media what we've been
forced to do as soon as you're gone. Hopefully that will keep
some of them from following you. Eventually, you will end up
at the airport. A ticket will be waiting for you."

Delilah nodded and couldn't help picturing all the footage
she'd seen of convicts being transported in much the same way.

"I'm really sorry," she said quietly, already mentally packing her bags. "I liked it here."

"And we loved having you. You've been such a great help, but there's no saying how long this will last. It's just too much for us to handle, and it's not fair to Jason. Hopefully it will be better for you in Utah."

Delilah nodded and forced a smile. "I'll go get my things." As she walked up the flight of stairs, she tucked a lock of her dark blonde hair behind her ear and told herself it was for the best. There were only three months left in the contract anyway. Despite the insane prices in New York City, she'd saved most of the money she'd earned. It wasn't as much as she expected to go home with, and she knew she'd never get a job in Big Fork that would make up the difference, but it wasn't like she was going home empty handed. And she couldn't deny that she longed to leave the city and get back to her boring hum-drum life. Besides, she hadn't seen Leif since just after he'd returned home from his mission in October. That was almost three months ago. Going home earlier meant that she wouldn't have to wait so long to see him again.

Leif and Delilah had dated since high school. After graduation, Delilah had enrolled in a small college a couple of towns away while Leif prepared for his mission. The September following their graduation he had left for Australia, and she had started counting the days until his return. While in school, Delilah got the idea of becoming a nanny. The opportunity to see more of the world than Southern Utah was appealing. Her first job was in Portland, Oregon and had lasted eight months. After that contract ended she'd applied for another position, this one in New York. The only drawback had been that it was for one year. It had taken a few days for her to make the decision to accept the job, since Leif would get home when she still had six months to go. But the salary eventually tipped the scales. When Leif returned from his mission in October, she'd taken a week off and come home to see him. It had been a powerful reunion, and by the time she boarded the plane back to New York, they had already begun making wedding plans.

They decided that Leif would get the training done for his Commercial Drivers License at the same time Delilah was finishing her nanny contract. CDL training required several long-haul road trips that could last up to eight weeks—he was half way through one right now and only had one more long haul to go to get his license. Once he was done with his training, he'd start working for the local trucking company in Big Fork, and he'd never have to do a long haul again.

She wished she could discuss all this with Leif, but he was driving across the Midwest, and they weren't answering the phones at the Jensen's. She'd managed to keep him up to date with numerous e-mails that he checked at Internet-ready truck stops—but e-mail was a poor substitute for hearing his voice. As she pulled her duffle bag out of the closet, she tried to make sense of why Sam Hendricks had picked her.

☆★☆

"Why did I pick Delilah? Can't I just ask someone else?" Sam said with just a hint of a whine in his voice. "Whoever I ask will accept, everyone will forget all about this Delilah person, and it will all become a distant memory."

Cody was shaking his head long before Sam finished. "That option has been tried in the public tribunal already. You'll be labeled a quitter if you ask someone else, and they'd be second choice anyway, and no girl wants that. You've got to find a way to make this girl accept. You might be the most sought after actor in Hollywood, but you still have the screw-ups of your past to reckon with, not to mention several failed relationships. People love dirty laundry, and you, my friend, have just been hung out to dry."

"How can public opinion change so fast? Five days ago everyone wanted to be my date. Now everyone hates me?"

"Love and hate are both four-letter words," Cody said. "They just want the juice. You gave them more than they bargained for, and you have to figure out how to quench their thirst."

The blasted phone rang again and Sam swore. Cody picked it up. "Yeah . . . Really? . . . When?" He twisted his wrist and looked at his watch before meeting Sam's eyes and giving him a thumbs-up sign. "We'll be there."

"Delilah's flying to Utah this afternoon, and I've arranged for you to talk to her for a few minutes at the airport."

Sam took a breath and stared at the floor. Finally he looked up. "I don't know how to handle this kind of rejection, Cody. I'm used to having women throw themselves at me—what do I say to her? How do I convince her to accept?"

Cody shook his head and shrugged his shoulders. "Just be yourself."

Sam rolled his eyes, *So much for good advice.* "I'm an actor," he said as he grabbed his Scandia suede coat off the back of the couch where he had flung it. "I don't know how to be myself."

★★★

Delilah allowed herself to be whisked into a car and driven around for two hours before finally being let out at the underground airport parking area reserved for celebrities and government officials. The car had made several stops along the way, meeting up with the other cars in order to reclaim her luggage. She stepped out of the car and took a deep breath as she scanned the area to make sure no one was going to jump out and thrust a microphone in her face. At three o'clock she would be driven across the tarmac to the plane, seated in first class, and taken away from this place. Her parents were driving from Big Fork to pick her up in Salt Lake, and then she hoped all of this would go away.

The driver loaded her bags onto a luggage cart and led her to the underground entrance. They wound their way through numerous halls, passing several doorways, until they finally met up with a Delta Airlines employee. He smiled warmly and took over as Delilah's guide. Delilah thanked the driver, and the Delta guy took over pushing the luggage cart. After a little while, the employee stopped at a door and told her to wait inside. She thanked him, entered the small room, and collapsed on the hard plastic chair. If only she were back in Utah already.

It was still difficult to comprehend the spinning top that was now her life. Even deep analysis of the circumstances didn't help her make sense of what had happened over the last five days. She leaned her head back and took a deep breath as she wondered what Leif was doing right now. He'd been in Michigan when he last e-mailed her. She wondered what state he was in now and wished she was going home to him. Unfortunately, he would be on the road for another three weeks. With a sigh she stretched her arms above her head and ran her fingers through her hair, massaging her scalp in hopes of releasing some of the tension she felt in every muscle of her body. After a couple minutes of pampering, she opened her eyes and blinked fast. Standing in front of her was none other than Sam Hendricks.

"Hi," he said with his Hollywood smile. She wanted to slap it off of his face.

"Oh, for heaven's sake," she muttered as she sat up straight and shook her head. She narrowed her eyes and crossed her arms over her chest. "What are you doing here?"

"I just came to talk."

"Yeah, right," she countered as her anger flared. "Do you realize what a mess you've made for me? I've been fired from my job, and my fiancé is driving across the country listening to reports of all this on the radio. The kid I used to care for is petrified of answering the door at his own home, and he's now without a nanny at all. Mr. Jensen is being hounded at work, and I'm having to sneak back to Utah as if I did something wrong. I did nothing! I took a kid to the park, and you'd think I committed a felony."

Sam just watched her, and she doubted he'd heard a word of it. "Well, it hasn't been a picnic for me, either," he said, putting his hands on his hips. "I'm getting lambasted because of you. I'm sorry about your little job and everything, but this is my whole life. I'm a laughing-stock when I should be soaking in adoration. I've been nominated for best actor—BEST

ACTOR—and now I'm the main topic of Leno jokes."

Delilah bolted to her feet and glared up at him. He was only about five inches talker than she was, and she'd have given anything for a pair of six inch platform shoes right now. It would be much more fitting if she was literally looking d own on him. "You have got to be kidding me," she said. "Are you really that shallow? You asked a girl out, and she said no. Big deal. The mere fact that this country even cares makes me wonder about the entire social climate of this nation. Two days from now this will be replaced by some new scandal, and you will go on your merry way, spending your millions and getting your little golden statues. I, on the other hand, will still be without a job that I desperately needed. You'll find some clever way to show this in a way the American people like, and your life won't change a bit."

"What?" Sam said after a two second pause. "This is my life, my whole life. What people think about me and what they say is my world and it just exploded. It might seem silly to you, but it's everything to me. You have no idea what it's like to live under the camera lens, to be judged and appraised all the time."

"Baloney! I grew up in a small town—there is no smaller microscope than that one."

Sam paused and cocked his head. "Did you just say 'baloney'?"

Delilah clenched her jaw and groaned. "This is so stupid!" she said, raising her arms and dropping them. "What are you doing here, other than trying to bring me to tears over your sad, pathetic life?"

Sam let out a deep breath. "I want you to reconsider my invitation. If you say yes, it will be better for both of us. I'll send you anywhere in the world for the next month, you'll get a make-over, you can go shopping to your heart's content, and I'll pay for every penny. On Oscar night, you come with me, and then we're done—through—finito. I'll never bug you again. Just come with me, help me turn this around."

"No way," she said quietly. "I hate the world you live in, and I don't want to be a part of it for even one silly little night."

Sam paled. "Silly little night? We're talking about the Oscars!"

"Yes, I know. The silliest little night I've ever heard of. Hollywood spends enough on clothes to feed a small country in order to judge one another for no real reason. They choose who *they* think is the best, and then they go party it up and spend a week with a hangover trying to remember who their date was. I don't want to be a part of it."

"I can't believe you just said that."

"Well, believe it, 'cause I did. I don't want to go."

Sam looked like he was ready to roar. The veins in his neck were bulging, but at least he wasn't trying to speak anymore. He seemed to realize it was a lost cause. The door opened, and they both looked up to see a man enter. Delilah recognized him as one of the men who had been with Sam that day in the park.

"I'm Cody Jenkes, Sam's personal assistant," the man said to Delilah. Then directing his comments to Sam, he asked, "How's it going?"

Sam just shook his head and turned to look at the wall, likely taking deep breaths and counting to ten. Delilah rolled her eyes. He was unbelievable.

Cody turned back to Delilah and smiled. His expression wasn't nearly as plastic as Sam's, but she still didn't trust him. "I know this has created problems for you, Ms. Glenshaw, and we really do apologize. We got carried away and handled this whole thing badly. However, now we all find ourselves in a mess, and I only see one way to get out of it."

"To have me say yes," she finished for him.

"Exactly," Cody said with a nod. "We're prepared to make it worth your while. We'll fly you—"

"I know, I know. Anywhere I want to go, let me shop for whatever crap I can't live without, and dress me up like a Barbie Doll. Not only am I not interested, I don't want to be interested. I don't live in the world Mr. Hendricks is from, and I don't want to. I have the right to say no. I've said it, and you need to leave me alone now."

She looked at Sam. His stupid hair was pulled back in a

ponytail, and his expression of frustration and annoyance caused her to harden toward him even more. Delilah had always had a stubborn streak, but she doubted she'd ever met anyone that brought it out so strongly. There was just something about him that made her want to tighten her defenses and prove herself the stronger and smarter of the two of them. From what she'd seen so far, she doubted it would be that hard to do.

"Is there any way at all that we can persuade, bribe, encourage, or beg you to do this?" Cody asked.

She looked at Sam again and realized just how sad his life was. This really was a big deal to him. It was so pathetic. This Richie Rich, who had zero hold on reality, really looked at this as a major trial in his life. It was so sad.

And then she had an idea.

She looked away for a few moments, and the idea grew and grew until a sweet smile of satisfaction spread across her face. When she looked up, both men were watching her.

"I'll make you a deal," she said, directing her comments to Sam. There was little doubt that her "deal" would be refused, but then they couldn't accuse her of being inflexible.

"Anything," Sam said in a hopeful voice as color seemed to return to his face.

"The Oscars are what, three weeks away?"

"Four."

"Even better," she said with a grin. "My parents own a dairy farm in Big Fork, Utah. We have sixty cows that we milk twice a day. We also grow hay on thirty-five acres of land. You want me to cross the gap between our worlds for one night. I don't know a thing about your world, and I really don't want to. But, if you'll be willing to cross that same gap for two weeks, I'll be your date."

"Huh?" Sam said with a confused expression that seemed to say, "What does this have to do with anything?"

Delilah continued, "You come to my parents' house for two weeks. You'll work the farm with me and my family and learn about my world—the world that doesn't get made into movies and adventure series. If you can do it for two weeks, without anyone in the media finding out about it, I'll go to the Oscars with you."

"Live on a dairy farm in Utah for two weeks?" he asked.

"Yes, and you come alone." She looked at Cody then back at Sam. "No valets, no drivers, bodyguards, cell phones, or pagers. You bring one suitcase of clothing and a good pair of work gloves. We have equipment and fences to repair in addition to the twice daily milking and cleaning up of sixty cows. Thanks to you, and your dumb idea of asking me to go with you, I've lost my job and I'm going home. That means I get to help put things in order for the spring, and we can always use an extra pair of hands."

"So it would be kind of like *The Simple Life* with Paris Hilton," Cody said.

"Except that it's thirty degrees in Big Fork. No one is going to be wearing bikinis or setting up photo ops for you. This is about you living real life. It's not a reality show."

Cody was deep in thought for a few seconds. "So Sam comes and lives with you for two weeks, and you'll accept the invitation?"

Sam turned his head slowly and stared at Cody with his mouth open. "You're not actually considering this?" he asked, sounding shocked. "I have interviews to do, talk shows to circuit—scripts to read! I'm not going to rot on some farm in Utah."

Cody turned to look at Sam. "Those interviews and talk shows are going to eat you alive after all this. I think milking cows sounds much less dangerous."

Sam shook his head. "This is ridiculous."

Delilah nodded. "You're right. It is." She headed for the door, smiling to herself that her little game had worked. She'd known all along that Sam would never agree. And now they could all move on with their lives. She'd given her conditions, and they had made their choice. But she couldn't help adding one last barb as she neared the door. "You couldn't handle it, anyway."

As she put her hand on the doorknob, Sam spoke again.

"Oh, I can handle it," he said with all the cocky pomp she should have expected.

She took a breath and turned around to face him again. A shiver of warning coursed down her spine, but she couldn't back down to him—his arrogance was infuriating. "No, you can't—you said it yourself."

"No, I said I didn't want to—not that I couldn't do it."

"Same thing," she said with a cocky grin of her own. This man was exasperating.

Cody looked from one to the other for a few seconds. "I don't think we have any choice," he said to both of them. "It's the only way to get you back in America's good graces. If handled correctly, this could be a very good thing for all of us."

Delilah froze for half a second. Was he serious? Or just trying to call her bluff? In the next instant she decided that she would play it to the end. All she had to do was meet Sam's eyes to get all the motivation she needed to continue. "No one can ever know about it," Delilah said, sounding very sincere even though her heart was pounding, and a million questions buzzed through her brain. But she didn't hesitate to continue. "Ever. If this goes public before the Oscars, I won't go. If it comes out afterwards, I'll sue you. I want you to promise that you'll never bring it up. This is my home, my family, and I'm not doing this so that you get publicity." But why was she doing it? She really wasn't sure, other than she didn't feel like she could back out now. What had she done?

"Telling the world that Sam Hendricks spent two weeks cleaning up manure in order to get a date is not the kind of publicity we want," Cody said. "You have nothing to worry about. One more thing, though. You're from Utah—are you Mormon?"

Delilah had been asked this question at least a hundred times since coming to New York. "Yes, I am."

"Well, I hope you won't get into preaching to Sam, here. We've agreed to not use this for publicity; you have to agree to not use it to proselytize."

Delilah shrugged. She probably wasn't being a very good

"member missionary," but she felt that the Church was too sacred to share with a man like Sam. "It's a deal. He's there to work, not to learn—we won't push anything."

It took another half an hour to work out the details of the situation. By the time they were done, Delilah's great idea had become a great big mess. But she'd pushed it this far; there was no choice but to follow through with it now. Cody left to schedule an emergency press conference at the Ritz Carlton Hotel, and her plane tickets were returned. The story they came up with was that she had said no because she thought her boyfriend would be angry. Since then they had spoken, and he said he understood and would never deny her this opportunity. Because of that, she had gladly accepted Sam's offer. In truth she'd just sent Leif an e-mail telling him what she'd done—she hoped he would understand. Once her refusal was explained, Cody would inform the press that she was going to a secluded island resort to rest up for the big event. To keep it all authentic, a body double would be sent to the island where she would play the part of "Delilah" while the real Delilah showed the famous Sam Hendricks how to milk a cow and mend barbed wire fences.

While they worked out the details, Sam tried to get out of it several times. However, Cody was excited about the idea and insisted that it was the only solution. To keep things quiet, Delilah and Sam would stay on her parents' farm for the duration of the visit. They would not go to town, and they would go nowhere in public. In fact, Delilah would have to hide out the entire time she was in Big Fork, even before Sam showed up. They couldn't very well have people figure out that she was home. With the gossip chains of a small town, one person finding out she was there would ruin everything.

Two hours later, Delilah held the press conference with a smiling Sam at her side. She gave the boyfriend story and did a pretty good job of convincing America that she was thrilled to have the opportunity of going to the Oscars. Then she was flown to Salt Lake on an unmarked private jet where her parents met her in the municipal portion of the airport set aside for private planes. Her parents were waiting for her when she stepped off the plane. Upon seeing them the tears finally came; she was so glad to be home. She'd only had the chance to explain briefly what was happening when she called them earlier. To say that they were surprised was an understatement. Luckily, they were supportive.

"When is he coming?" Mary, Delilah's mother, asked once they pulled into the southbound lane of I-15.

"Saturday," Delilah said. That was only five days from now. She must have lost her mind.

"Well," Mary said with a forced smile, "this should be fun."

Delilah looked out the window and watched everything whiz by as she wondered when the knot in her stomach would go away. *This is so insane!* she told herself over and over. Then again, ever since that fateful meeting in the park her life had been unrecognizable. Why not throw another log on the fire?

✵ Chapter Four ✵

Driving back from the press conference, Sam pouted as he attempted to distract himself by playing a game on his cell phone.

"I was wondering," Cody said casually, "if we shouldn't put a camera or two in the Glenshaw's house, just in case we get something really good."

Sam didn't look up from his phone, but he shook his head.

"You know someone is going to find out about this, Sam," Cody continued. "You're Sam Hendricks—you won't really be able to hide. If we have some footage, then, when it's discovered, we'll have something to show the world. All we need is one great moment, one thing we can—"

"No way," Sam said, still not looking up from his game as he continued to push buttons. "I never want anyone to know I did this—I still can't believe I agreed." He snapped the phone shut and looked at Cody. "The last thing I want is evidence."

"But just in case—"

"No," Sam said strongly. "Besides, we promised Delilah we wouldn't let anyone know."

"And we won't—unless they find out another way, and we have to defend ourselves."

"That doesn't make any sense," Sam said. "What would we be defending ourselves of? You just want to watch it and laugh at me the whole two weeks. I'm sure you can find something better to do. This will be forgotten as soon as I leave that stupid farm. No cameras. And if footage was ever discovered, Delilah would sue us, remember?"

"And we'd settle for a couple hundred grand," Cody said. "That's a fortune to her kind of people. And if it gave us the perfect shot, something we could spin into gold . . ."

"No," Sam said for the third time. "No cameras, not a word

to anyone. You are the only one on the planet that is going to know anything about this. Understood?"

Cody took a breath and let it out. "Okay," he said with a shrug. "You're the boss."

Sam nodded and started a new game, his eyebrows still pinched together. "Just make sure you don't forget that," he said.

Cody looked at him with slightly narrowed eyes but said nothing. Sam was too busy shooting alien aircraft to notice.

Cody waited until Sam settled down in the apartment before he handed him a script they'd received by messenger that morning and left him to his own mutterings of how "ridiculous" and "demeaning" this whole thing was. Cody said he was going out for coffee, but instead he went out to the car and made a phone call.

The other party picked up after two rings. They didn't introduce themselves—they didn't need to. Cody had been formulating this plan since Delilah first made the offer to have Sam go to Utah. With a few short phone calls—made while Sam was otherwise occupied—Cody put his plan into action. He had hoped that Sam would play along with his idea of the camera, that he would see the sense in the plan. But as usual, Sam couldn't see past his own nose. Cody had little doubt that Sam would play along eventually. Convincing Sam to do things Cody's way had occupied every moment of his life for over a year—this was no different. Cody was the one that made sure Sam smiled in the right places, that he said the right things, and shook the right hands. It was because of Cody, and a long line of personal assistants before him, that the world even liked Sam Hendricks. Cody wasn't sure what he'd use the footage for. Maybe he'd never need to. But the opportunity was too tempting to ignore.

"She's on her way," Cody said into the phone. "Her parents will be leaving soon to pick her up—it's a six hour drive there and back."

"Is there anyone else at the house?" asked the voice on the other end.

"I asked her a lot of questions under the guise of trying to plan for Sam. The house will be cleared out, but they have some hired help coming in to do the evening milking. Look out for paparazzi. They've been hanging out around town, but since the parents have refused to talk to anyone they've left the farm. But keep a sharp eye. We can't afford to have anyone find out about this . . . yet. And you need to be in and out in two hours to make sure you don't run into the evening workers. Can you do that?"

"Absolutely. We're almost there already."

"And make sure no one knows the camera's there. If they find it, we're in trouble."

"Not a problem. I'll call you when it's in so we can test the system."

"Good," Cody said with a triumphant smile. "Let's make sure we do a good job." He turned off his phone and tapped it against his chin. A mini-studio was being set up in the guest room of Sam's Malibu beach house—the room Cody stayed in. The camera was equipped with motion sensors so that it only filmed when people were in the room. The footage would then be recorded in Malibu, where Cody could watch it whenever he pleased. He couldn't help but smile. He was so much smarter than Sam gave him credit for. This would prove it once and for all.

For the next five days, Sam did twice as many interviews as he'd planned. The shows who had him scheduled during the time he would be in Utah were given the option of a taped interview or nothing at all. Most of them chose wisely. He taped two or three interviews every day. Cody told him that with the media frazzle they'd created about Delilah's refusal and then acceptance, coupled with the doubled up interviews, his disappearance wouldn't be noticed. He'd be back in his Malibu beach house before anyone wondered if he was missing.

Sam let Cody go on and on with the plans and arrangements. No matter how many times Cody explained himself, though, it was hard to ignore the fact that while Cody sat in a lounge chair taking messages, Sam was going to be milking cows in Utah. Shaking his head, he forced himself to remember all the reasons he had to do this, but it still wasn't making much sense. There had to be some other way to pull this off.

But Cody disagreed, and Cody had never led him astray before. Of all the assistants Sam had had over the years, Cody was the best. He didn't mind being with Sam all the time. He didn't mind making coffee in the morning or doing Sam's laundry on the housekeeper's day off. All of Sam's other assistants eventually got whiny about the twenty-four hour companionship or not having their own place. Sam hated that. The first and foremost requirement of a good assistant was absolute loyalty—like a good dog. That's why he liked Cody so much. He was perfectly content using Sam's house and car. Sam liked it best that way. In his opinion, an assistant needed to help him live his life, not go off finding a life of his own. Cody could be trusted. Sam's best interest was Cody's only goal in life. All that taken into account, maybe Utah wouldn't be that bad.

The night before the big day arrived. Cody loaded Sam's only bag into the Lexus while Sam looked over his beach house one last time. He wished he could take it with him. Rather than run into media problems at the airport, Cody suggested that they drive—it was only ten hours, he said. Sam grumbled like a fifteen-year-old, but went along.

They started driving at eleven o'clock that night, and Sam fell asleep around midnight. When he awoke the next morning, the congested freeways and high-rise office buildings of California had disappeared. In their place was a narrow two-lane highway, lots of sagebrush, and an occasional gas station. Sam slumped in his heated, leather seat and wished he could fall asleep again and wake up two weeks from now. He was trying to be a good sport, wanting to prove Delilah wrong about his ability to "pull it off," but with each passing mile he was dreading it more and more.

"Where are we?" Sam asked, hoping Cody wouldn't say they were almost there. He had been picturing a beautiful ranch overlooking red rock arches dotted with bike trails and swimming pools—this place looked like the footage he'd seen of the middle east.

"We're almost there," Cody said.

Sam groaned and tried to trade his mental image of luxurious surroundings for . . . nothingness. It wasn't easy.

Cody continued, "We'll be there in half an hour. Are you ready?"

"As ready as I'll ever be," Sam said, and he meant every word. He had a feeling that this very moment was going to be the highlight of the next two weeks of his life.

Twenty minutes later they made the final turn in a long list of detailed instructions onto a gravel driveway. Fastened to the front gate was a sign that read "No Trespassing. Violators will be prosecuted. Media people will be shot on sight."

Delilah was still in the middle of morning chores when she heard the sound of tires on gravel. Her dad had taken her mom to a doctor appointment in the next town over as soon as most of the work was done. The milkings were normally manned by five workers, but because Delilah was here only the two most trustworthy were still helping out. Rhett had promised them a bonus for the extra work and for not telling anyone what was happening on the farm. Eric and Miguel had worked with the Glenshaws for years, and they could be trusted. However, half of the bonus Rhett had promised them came out of the money Delilah had been saving. It had been her hope that when she and Leif got married, she would have enough to put a down payment on a house. With the shortened contract and having to pay half the bonus, it wasn't shaping up that way. But when she complained, her father reminded her that this had been her idea. Her STUPID idea.

Eric and Miguel were gone until this evening, which meant Delilah was Sam Hendrick's sole welcoming party. Her stomach flipped, and she closed her eyes while she said a little prayer. She'd regretted her impetuous negotiation a million times since she offered it, but there was no one to blame other than herself and no choice but to try and make the best of it— or the worst of it for Sam.

In order to keep up the ruse that she was staying at some exotic island resort, Delilah had stayed home the entire time. She didn't go to town for any reason—not to see old friends, not to grab a plate of French fries with gravy at the diner, not even to go to church. She'd simply stayed home and helped with chores, worked on her wedding plans, and thought of a hundred things she should have done differently.

A car door slammed, and she knew she was out of time. The dreaded moment had arrived, and it was up to her to make sure she stuck to her guns and made her point. That was what this was all about in the first place—making a point. It was time to get to work.

"Hello," she shouted as she exited the barn and pulled her gloves off, stuffing them into the pocket of her insulated coveralls. The two men looked at her, and Cody waved back. Sam was looking around as if he'd landed on another planet. For just an instant she imagined what she must look like right now—her hair was pulled into a sloppy ponytail, her coveralls, two sizes too big, were filthy, and her rubber work boots were caked in cow manure. *What a great first impression* she thought. But this was going to be Sam's life for the next fourteen days. He may as well get used to it.

She reached them a few seconds later and pushed aside her feelings of self-consciousness. Instead of trying to repair herself a little, she lifted her chin and tried to reflect the kind of irritating arrogance she'd seen in Sam each time they had met. She didn't bother putting out her dirty, sweaty hand; she doubted either of them wanted to shake it.

She forced a smile. "So you found the place okay?" she asked.

"The directions you gave me were perfect," Cody said.

Delilah nodded. "The thermometer on the side of the barn says it's thirty-five degrees today, but it feels colder because of the wind." She looked at Sam and felt her first bubble of triumph.

He looked absolutely miserable as he tried to keep his long hair from blowing in his face. "I hope you brought a good coat," she continued.

Sam just nodded and pulled his light jacket tighter around himself.

She decided to give them a quick tour of the property closest to the house. When they finished outside, they ventured indoors and Delilah showed Sam his room. It had been her brother Daniel's room until he'd left for his mission one year ago. Cody dropped Sam's bag and coat just inside the doorway.

He stared at the twin bed and turned to look at her. "You've got to be kidding!" It was the first thing he'd said since his arrival.

"You don't like it?" she asked with raised eyebrows and feigned surprise.

He looked back at the room, moving his eyes slowly from one piece of old chipped furniture to another. Apparently he was overwhelmed to the point of speechlessness.

Delilah couldn't suppress her smile—this was starting to get fun. "It was either this or the hide-a-bed downstairs."

"It'll be fine," Cody said, clapping Sam on the back and turning him away from his less-than-posh accommodations. "Let's take a look at the kitchen—so he knows where to find things."

Delilah nodded and led them to the kitchen. Sam glowered as he scanned the room. Cody seemed to take in every detail. Delilah looked around the room too, trying to see it through their eyes. New but plain cabinets, dark gray Formica counters, and black marbled linoleum on the floor. A potted herb garden filled one windowsill, and the other held a miscellaneous collection of odds and ends that had no place of their own. The kitchen was nice compared to what it used to look like, but it looked cheap and overly simple next to these two men. Their clothes likely cost more than the entire renovation. The realization prompted her to lift her chin and stand up straight. It wasn't fancy, but it was solid and it was her home. She would stand proud and not let herself feel small about any of this.

"This is a lovely kitchen," Cody said as he became particularly interested in the expansive collection of cookie jars above the fridge on the far side of the room.

"My mom collects cookie jars," Delilah said as a way to explain why every inch of horizontal space in the room was crowded by the ceramic creations. Twice a year Mary would take them down and wash them before putting them right back up there. Delilah thought it was cute for her mom to have a hobby, but she herself thought it looked like a garage sale waiting to happen. Cody took a few steps closer and turned his head as he looked from jar to jar.

"Mom had the kitchen redone last year," Delilah continued, wondering what it was about the Snoopy cookie jar that had Cody so engaged. "It doesn't match the rest of the house, but mom hopes to update the other rooms a little at a time."

Cody finished his examination of Snoopy and turned to her with a wide smile. "She's got excellent taste."

There was a moment of silence as everyone seemed to be trying to come up with something to say. Finally Cody spoke up. "I guess I better go."

Sam looked at him with a composed expression that was too well done to be sincere. The men walked out to the car, and Delilah wondered what amount of money Sam would offer for her to call this off. Right now she'd probably take a chocolate shake and call it even. She wiped off the countertop and imagined Sam begging Cody to take him back to California.

After a few minutes, Delilah went outside to try and find her new field hand. Sam was standing in the middle of the driveway with his hands in the pockets of his designer jeans, looking lost and forlorn. For just a moment, she felt sorry for taking him away from the world he knew—but it didn't last long. He owned a house in Malibu, an apartment in New York, and probably a dozen condos all over the world. She doubted he'd ever done his own laundry or wondered how he'd pay the water bill. It was her self-appointed job to give him the only dose of reality he would likely ever get. She took that role seriously and promised herself, in that moment, that she would do whatever it took to make sure he "got it." This was a lesson he would never repeat—she was sure of that. It was up to her to make sure it stuck to him and never washed off.

As soon as Sam heard the crunch of gravel beneath her feet, he turned and smiled. It was so bright and so sincere that she stopped, surprised by the sudden change in his mood. Then she remembered that he *was* nominated for best actor for a reason.

"So, where do I start?" he said, clapping his hands together and smiling as if they were about to jump on a jet ski. She took his attitude as a challenge.

"Well," she said with a casual grin. "Why don't we start by washing down the floor of the barn?"

Sam made a sweeping bow and winked in her direction. "After you."

She led him to the barn door and watched his nose wrinkle at the strong smell of cow manure. "There's always an eastern wind out here, so this barn was built up wind. You can't smell much until you get real close—it was great engineering." She couldn't help but smile as she opened the door and let him in.

The barn had an aisle that separated two gated sections of cows. The gate was made of pipes welded together in such a way as to allow human access to the feed troughs that ran the length of the gates, but didn't allow the cows to run rampant. She explained that this was where the cows spent most of their time during the winter months. Coveralls similar to her own hung on the wall, and she suggested Sam put some on over his clothes. Sam made no move toward them, although he looked them over in detail.

"The cows get to wander in the pasture most of the year, but it's just too cold right now. We keep a bed of straw on the far sides of the stall areas and the feed on the interior side. That way they don't mess up their bed, since they usually poop while they eat." She glanced at Sam. He repaired his look of disgust as soon as he realized she was watching. "When it's milking time, we take the cows in two groups out that far door into the milking barn—but I'll show you all that tonight."

She pointed out the long, and not so clean, hoses at the far side of the barn. There were two of them rolled onto the wall, one for each row of stalls. "Why don't you take the stalls on the right and I'll take the stalls on the left. Just start at the top and hose down the floor. There's just enough slope to help carry the water to those drains at the end. We wash it down every day, otherwise it really starts to stink in here."

He managed to smile at her joke while his eyes followed the floor to a row of floor grates not far from where they stood. Then he looked up and met her eye. "No problem."

"Glad to hear it," Delilah responded. She grabbed her hose, turned the water on, and started spraying through the metal gates that kept the cows corralled. She was almost ten feet down when she glanced over her shoulder just in time to see Sam spray too hard. The water pressure caused the manure to explode, covering his shoes and jeans. He swore under his breath, and she looked away before he knew she'd seen what happened. She had to pinch her lips closed to keep from laughing.

When she finished spraying down her side of the barn, she looked back to see that Sam wasn't quite half done with his side. He was wet from mid chest down and had manure all over his shoes. For a moment, she considered taking pity on the poor guy and helping him. Then she realized that since he wasn't doing a good job she would likely have to redo it anyway. She wasn't about to let him off the hook just because he wasn't any good. What would that teach him?

"I'm going to get some lunch," she said as she passed him to roll up her hose. "I'll see you inside."

He seemed to be concentrating too hard to respond. She left it at that and peeled off her coveralls before hanging them back up on the wall. She smiled the whole way back to the house.

Forty-five minutes passed before she heard the back door open. She'd had time to shower, get dressed, dry and braid her hair, eat lunch, and clean the kitchen.

"Take off your dirty clothes in the mud room before you come in the house," she called to him.

"Everything I have on is dirty," he yelled back.

"Then strip down in the half bath and grab a robe off the

door. Next time you work in the barn, put on a pair of coveralls."

She couldn't hear his response, but she guessed it was colorful and full of four-letter words. She put the detergent in the door of the dishwasher and shut it before starting the cycle. The watery churning sound filled the room.

"Oh, and throw your dirty clothes into the washer and get the machine going before anything dries."

Delilah finished wiping down the countertops just as he came into the kitchen wrapped in an old blue robe they kept in that bathroom specifically for "amateurs."

"I don't know how to run the washer thing," he admitted.

"Okay," she said cheerily as she threw the washrag into the sink. He didn't follow her, and she turned to look at him when she reached the doorway that led to the mudroom. "I'm only going to show you once."

"You're going to make this a lot of fun, aren't you."

She cocked her head to the side and gave him her best impression of his own fake smile that she was coming to know so well. "That's what life is all about, Sam. Having fun rules every moment of every day around here."

He followed, shaking his head. She went over the basics of doing one's own laundry. He pretended that he understood, but she had little doubt she would be showing him again despite the fact that she'd already told him she wouldn't. They returned to the kitchen, and Sam sat down at the table before looking around. Not seeing whatever he was looking for, he finally just looked at her.

"What?" Delilah asked. It was her night to do dinner, and she needed to get it started. She pulled out the ingredients to make enchiladas.

"Didn't you say you were making lunch?" Sam asked as she plopped a can of green chilies on the counter.

"Yeah, *my* lunch."

"You didn't make anything for me?"

"Nope."

His jaw clenched just a little bit, but he managed a nod. "I assume I have permission to use your food to fix my own?"

"Mi casa es su casa," she said. "You are welcome to use, eat, and borrow anything we have whenever you need it. The exceptions are things found in private bedrooms and anything that runs on gas—you have to ask for those. Other than that, you have free reign."

He didn't seem all that grateful and after a few seconds he got up and went to the fridge. "Where are your parents?"

"They went to Cedar City; that's about forty-five miles from here. They'll be back soon."

Sam stared at the contents of the fridge. He didn't seem inspired. "Don't you have any water?" he asked after a few seconds.

"That big hole in the counter next to you is called a sink. That metal thing is called a faucet. If you lift up the lever, water comes out of it."

"I meant do you have any drinking water."

"Oh," Delilah said with a nod as if she understood now. "You can get a glass out of the cupboard, catch some of the water in it, and drink it directly from the glass."

Sam turned and looked at the faucet as if he'd never seen one before. "You drink tap water?" he asked dryly.

"Kind of primitive, I know, but well, it's the best we have." It was so hard for her not to laugh.

Finally he shut the fridge door, apparently giving up on having bottled spring water appear on the shelves. "I can't even think about eating when I smell this bad."

"I know what you mean," she said as she began opening cans. "I shower three times a day sometimes, and I still can't seem to get the smell out."

Sam looked up at her with an expression that seemed to border on longing—as if her admission made him feel better. She wasn't sure if she liked that. Refusing to look at him, she busied herself with dinner preparations. The worst thing she could do was give in and be sympathetic, but it wasn't in her nature to be so cold either. It was a battle she didn't know how to fight so she changed the subject. "Let me tell you how we do the milkings, then when we get out there you'll have something to reference. The first thing we do is wash off the udders really well, we can't have any manure or anything on them when we hook them up to the pump. Then . . ."

✮ Chapter Five ✮

Delilah's parents, Rhett and Mary Glenshaw, arrived home about an hour later, after Delilah had left Sam totally disgusted with her detailed and slightly exaggerated descriptions of cow milking. Sam had finally escaped to take a shower, returning to the kitchen just a few minutes after Rhett and Mary walked in.

Rhett was a bear of a man, with hands the size of dinner plates and thick muscled shoulders. He had dark hair, bushy eyebrows, and a perpetual five o'clock shadow. He no longer worked the farm full-time; instead he focused on his insurance business that he ran from home. Farm work had taken its toll on his back, much as desk work had now taken a toll on his growing belly. But he was a handsome man with a quiet disposition of authority and piercing blue eyes very much like Delilah's. Mary was nearly a foot shorter than her husband, with hair that was mostly gray these days. In her youth she had boasted the same honey gold hair that Delilah now had. In fact, mother and daughter looked a lot alike. They both had round faces, high cheekbones, bright blue eyes, and engaging smiles.

Delilah made the introductions, and then Rhett offered to take Sam out on the tractor to see the property Delilah hadn't had a chance to show him. By the time they returned, Sam seemed to be in better spirits, and Rhett whispered, "He's not that bad," as he passed Delilah in the hall. She narrowed her eyes and shook her head. He was Sam Hendricks—the enemy, although she wasn't quite sure why. But regardless of the reason, they were on opposing teams here, and she didn't like her father falling for his Hollywood charm. It couldn't work in her favor.

That evening the four of them sat down to Delilah's enchiladas. Dinner came complete with rice and authentic black beans. Once they sat, the three Glenshaws folded their arms and bowed their heads. Sam followed their lead but asked nothing about why they prayed. When the blessing had been offered, they lifted their heads and began eating. Delilah eyed Sam as she ate, waiting to hear some complaints, but he seemed to like it— although she noticed he pulled a face when he drank from his water glass; he didn't drink anything after that. At first it was awkwardly silent. Finally, Mary broke the ice.

"So, Sam, tell us a little about yourself."

Sam swallowed his rice. "Well, there's not much to tell that most people don't already know. My mom is Carol Cheney and my dad is Matthew Hendricks. They divorced when I was two, and I lived mostly with my mom."

"And that was in California?" Mary asked.

"Well, all over actually. My mom did a lot of movies when I was young. I traveled with her."

"It must be exciting to have seen so much of the world," Mary continued. Delilah began to feel concern over the interest she saw on her mother's face. "What's your favorite place that you've ever been?"

Sam took several moments to think that question through. "It would have to be the island of St. Barts. There's no place like that in the world. It's all sand and clubs and beautiful w—," he paused and looked at Delilah quickly. She raised an eyebrow and silently dared him to continue. He chickened out. "And beautiful *windows* that show enchanting ocean views."

"Rhett took me on a Caribbean cruise for our twentieth wedding anniversary. We went to Grand Cayman. Is that like St. Barts?"

"Pretty close," Sam agreed. Delilah didn't like how comfortable he was getting.

"Except St. Barts has nude beaches, right Sam?" Delilah cut in.

Sam looked at her with feigned innocence. "I wouldn't know. I don't go to those kinds of beaches."

"Of course not," Mary said, patting his hand as if to sooth his offended soul. She gave Delilah a reprimanding look.

Mary went on with her questions—her casualness should have alerted her family to where this conversation was going. "Have you ever met Neil Diamond?"

Rhett and Delilah looked at one another. Why hadn't they seen this coming? She'd just been warming up for the kill. If Mary had one weakness in the whole world it was her passionate crush on Neil Diamond.

"Sure have," Sam said, not noticing the way everyone was anticipating his answer.

Delilah groaned and Rhett started eating faster. Mary's eyes went wide.

"Really?" she breathed.

"Yeah, my mom knows him. I went to his place in Florida once when I was fourteen."

That was it—Delilah knew she'd lost this round. A smile broke out on Mary's face that Delilah didn't recognize. In a matter of moments Mary was dragging them all through memories of her college days, telling them about waiting in line for two days to get tickets for a Neil Diamond concert. Delilah had heard the story a hundred times. Mary owned every album he'd ever produced on 8-track, record, tape, and CD. Every television concert he'd ever done had been recorded and sat next to family movies on the shelves of their entertainment center. Transferring the concerts to DVD for preservation purposes was Mary's latest project.

For the next ten minutes, they were forced to sit and hear about how she almost got to go backstage, how she joined his fan club for a few years and, most recently, how she had lost an eBay auction for a signed T-shirt from the very concert she had attended all those years ago. She'd been outbid at the last minute and was still very bitter.

Sam listened with the intent of a seasoned Hollywood actor. He made all the right comments in all the right places, and when she finished her eBay recitation he broke in. "You know," he said coyly, risking the tiniest of sparing glances with Delilah before continuing, "I have a signed copy of the Rolling Stones magazine he was on the cover of—you know, the one in 1976."

"You don't," Mary said breathlessly. Her fork clattered to the table.

"I do," he confirmed with a slow nod. "And when I get back to Malibu I'll send it to you, as a thank-you for your hospitality."

Mary's mouth moved, but no words came out. Tears started to form in her eyes. Sam just grinned wider.

"Well, I'm done," Rhett announced as he stood, smiling at his wife and shaking his head. He looked at Sam. "One of the reasons she married me was because I look a little like Neil Diamond."

Sam laughed good-naturedly and leaned back in his chair. "You know, you do look like him."

Delilah rolled her eyes. Her dad didn't look anything like Neil Diamond. It was a joke he'd been telling for thirty years. Mary was still speechless.

"Come on out to the barn when you're finished, Sam," Rhett said as he clapped Sam on the back. "We'll show you how to work the milking machines."

"You've got five minutes," Delilah added as she stood and took her plate to the sink.

"Now, Delilah, be nice," Mary warned.

Delilah turned and stared at her mother, surprised at the reprimand. Mary continued. "Sam is our guest here. Treat him as you would any guest."

Delilah blinked. "Sam is here to work, Mom."

"But he is also our guest. You can show a little more courtesy."

Sam smiled and looked at her as if waiting for an apology. Fat chance.

"Sam will be happy to help with the dishes once the milking is done, won't you, Sam?"

His face fell just a little but was instantly repaired when Mary turned to look at him with a hopeful expression. Delilah passed by them, feeling satisfied once more. He had wormed his way into her mother's heart using Neil Diamond; let him try and get away from her now.

Eric and Miguel had already taken the first group of cows to the milking barn. They did their jobs as usual while Rhett showed Sam the various steps of the evening milking. Delilah did her own chores by herself. It was only her first day working with Sam, and she was already sick of being around him. When she had finished her chores in the barn more than two hours later, she headed for the house. Sam caught up to her a few yards away from the back door and made a grand display of opening it for her.

"Thank you," she said, even though she didn't want to.

"It's my pleasure," he cooed.

She rolled her eyes as she passed him.

"You love doing that, don't you?" he said.

"Doing what?" she asked as she hung her coat on the row of hooks just inside the back door.

Sam did an exaggerated impression of Delilah rolling her eyes. Then he looked at her and smiled.

"Whenever I do that, I'm saying, 'This guy is such a loser.'"

Sam shook his head and clicked his tongue. "Be nice or I'll tell Mom."

She stared at him pointedly and rolled her eyes with added dramatic flare.

He laughed and walked ahead of her into the kitchen. She took off her shoes and overheard him say, "Now, Mary, you were supposed to save those dishes for me to help with . . . you made apple pie . . . well I can't even remember the last time I had homemade apple pie . . . you know, Neil loves apple pie."

Delilah put her hands on her knees and let out a deep breath. This might not go as smoothly as she'd hoped. But she wasn't giving up. Tomorrow was a new day, and it started at five a.m. Sam didn't know that yet. She couldn't wait to tell him.

The next day was Sunday and Delilah grumbled about not being able to go to church. She hated having to hide in her own house. To compensate for her annoyance she was determined to make the day as miserable for Sam as possible. In a lot of ways he was like a little brother she could torment—she missed that part of her life. It was his fault all this was happening anyway. At promptly five o'clock, she banged on the door and smiled when she heard a thump indicating he'd rolled off the little bed.

"Time to get up!" she hollered.

The sounds that followed her announcement were likely expletives, but she couldn't make them out through the door. "Meet us in the barn," she continued before moving on.

Half an hour later she trudged through the morning darkness back to the house. She banged on his door again. "I told you to get up!" she yelled.

Silence.

She opened the door to find him rolled up in a Winnie-the-Pooh comforter. "Get up," she repeated.

"What time is it?" he asked, his voice muffled.

"Time to get up," she called back. "The deal is that you do your part, Sam. Now get up or call Cody to come and get you."

A well-muscled arm emerged from the tangle of the comforter and pulled it down. His hair was a mess, and his perfect face had seam lines pressed into it. He glanced at the clock on the side table. "It's not even six o'clock," he said with a groan as his head flopped back onto the mattress.

"And the cows are ready to be milked—come on."

She heard him cuss as she turned away, and spun promptly back to face him. "And don't swear," she said. "We have a rule that if anyone oversleeps, they have to wash the floor of the barn by themselves. I'll let you off the hook this morning, but only if you're there in five minutes."

Sam groaned again and sat up, still cocooned in the comforter. "Fine," he said in a grouchy tone. "I'll be out as soon as I'm done with my coffee."

"We don't drink coffee."

"I do."

Delilah folded her arms across her chest. "Well, we don't have any coffee. It's not allowed in our house. You can't go to town, and you have a hundred cows to milk. I think that sums it up. Get dressed. You have five minutes."

Sam entered the barn six minutes later with a look that

could kill. Delilah ignored his mood entirely while she and Rhett showed him what to do all over again. Not one simple task had been retained overnight. If he'd been a hired hand, he'd have been fired. He was exceptionally hesitant about touching the cows. If he had to touch them he became very stiff as if too much contact might burn his flesh or something. Milking took an extra hour thanks to his help. Rhett had to leave them to finish up in order to make it to church on time.

It was a long day, full of Delilah pouting and Sam taking deep breaths—or was it the other way around? The two of them said less than three words to one another the whole time Rhett and Mary were gone. When they returned, Sam picked up with the Neil Diamond trivia, but even Mary seemed to be getting her fill of it. During the afternoon, the Glenshaws watched a video about John Taylor and discussed the church lessons Delilah had missed. Sam took a nap.

Leif called from Louisiana that afternoon, and Delilah got to talk to him for over an hour—it was heavenly. In the last two and a half years, they had spent less than five days in one another's company. She missed him so much. Hearing his voice was like getting a massage. She could feel the tension drain out of her body. They talked about everything they could think of until his phone card warned them that he was nearly out of time. They said quick goodbyes and I love you's before she hung up. Tears threatened, and she hurried into her bedroom to fully experience the self-pity.

I just want this to be over and done, she thought to herself as she lay on the bed. She closed her eyes and played out the fantasy of her wedding day that was so close and yet so far away. Right now she'd give just about anything to be with Leif. Instead she was trapped in the company of Superstar Sam. She put a pillow over her face and screamed.

There were no extra chores today, and once Delilah got over her pity-party she couldn't help but get excited for tomorrow. She was sure by now that Sam thought every day consisted of a morning and evening milking, with eight free hours in between. No such luck. To keep her mind off of Leif and how much she missed him, she focused on how much fun tomorrow would be. Tomorrow was when the real work would begin.

The next morning Sam didn't come out to the barn after she banged on his door. She went back at five-thirty and informed him that he was on floor duty by himself today.

"Then what's the motivation for me to get up?" he shouted through the door. "I may as well sleep longer."

"Every fifteen minutes adds another chore," Delilah yelled.

"The grates need to be cleaned out today—you'll get that, too, if you don't hurry."

He decided to really test her limits and ended up having to wash the floors, clean the grates, and put fresh straw in the stalls. He muttered under his breath the whole time and made a huge mess of the straw. Delilah had to stay and supervise his work despite the fact that she'd gotten up on time. She seriously questioned her punishments—but what else was she supposed to do? He had to learn that it was better to get up on time.

After Sam finished his extra chores, they headed into the house. Miguel and Eric had been gone for hours, and Rhett was out meeting with a client. Delilah was taking off her shoes inside the back door when Sam let himself in and began to follow suit. He seemed to be hurrying, but he still had a scowl every time he looked at her.

"It's not my fault you slept in," she said in response to his unspoken cursings.

He shook his head as if he didn't believe her. "I've got a taped interview to watch. What time is *Oprah* on out here?"

"I wouldn't know," Delilah said dryly as she stretched her arms over her head and twisted her back in hopes of working out the stiffness. It was nearly one o'clock and she was starving. She wouldn't let Sam come in for breakfast until he finished his chores. She sure hoped she would be a better parent because of this experience.

"Well, do you have a *TV Guide*?" he asked with irritation.

Delilah shrugged. "Who needs a *TV Guide* when you don't have a TV?"

Sam froze in the process of removing his shoe and turned his head to look at her. "What?" he said. His voice was nearly a whisper, and Delilah felt her spirits rise. The shoe fell from his hands and thumped to the floor.

"Well, we have a TV," she said. He relaxed until she continued, "But the satellite system got messed up last year, and we haven't gotten it fixed—so we can only watch movies."

"You don't watch TV?"

Delilah shrugged. "We're usually too busy to watch TV."

Sam continued to stare. "I have half a dozen taped interviews playing this week."

"Well, call in the cavalry!" she said sarcastically. "You were there when they were taped, surely you won't be overly surprised with your answers."

"You don't understand," he said with clenched teeth. His other shoe dropped to the floor, and he just sat there for a few moments.

Delilah stood and turned to face him. "I agree with you there," she said with feigned sincerity. "I can't imagine the pressure you must feel being the center of the universe—it must be exhausting."

"Do you treat everyone like this?" Sam asked.

"Nope," she said with a smile. "Only people who ask for it."

Sam shook his head and clenched his teeth. "Do you realize the Sonics are playing the Lakers Friday night? Are you telling me I won't get to see the game?"

Delilah leaned toward him until their heads were only six inches apart. "I will speak very slowly so that you don't miss any of the information. We . . . don't . . . have . . . television."

Sam let out a breath and looked at the floor.

Delilah smiled and shrugged her shoulders. "Sorry," she said with fake sympathy.

Sam slumped on the bench and Delilah left him to wallow, hoping her dad wouldn't tell him that he still watched the games over the Internet. She wanted Sam to suffer a little longer before he figured it out.

A while later Sam came into the kitchen where Delilah was

looking through a bridal magazine. She quickly closed the magazine, not wanting to start a conversation about her upcoming wedding. It was a sacred thing and one he would have little appreciation for, she was sure. She had already showered and leftover enchiladas were heating in the oven for lunch.

"Can I help you?" she asked.

"Actually, I have something for you," Sam said with a grin. He looked very pleased with himself. The change in his mood, from sullen and depressed to gratified gift-giver made her regard him with suspicion. He handed her a large gold box, the kind one would get from a high-end department store. She pictured spring-loaded snakes jumping out when she took off the lid.

"What's this?"

"Open it," he said with a wave of his hand. "It's for the Oscars."

She took the box and removed the lid. No snakes, just white tissue paper. After pulling back the paper she pulled a very small blue dress from the box. She immediately loved it and hated it at the same time. The fabric was divine and moved through her fingers like liquid. She could only imagine what it would feel like on her skin. However, half of the dress was missing. She reluctantly returned it to the box.

"Sam, I can't wear that," she said. The disappointment in her voice was sincere.

"Why not?" he asked, lifting it himself and showing it to her as if she didn't understand what it was.

"It's Versace. I had it made for you."

"It's lovely," she said. "But there's not enough of it."

"Well, I know you might need to lose a few pounds to make it fit right but we've—"

"What did you just say?" she broke in.

"I . . . uh . . . what I meant was that this dress is a size ten, so . . ." He wisely stopped speaking.

Delilah leaned forward, not believing what she'd just heard.

"Did you just tell me to lose some weight?"

Wisdom prevailed, and Sam said nothing.

"Let me make a few things very clear," she said in slow,

calculated words. "I am not a Barbie for you to dress up. My weight is not a topic for discussion and I am not planning to lose any. I can't wear that dress because it has no back and no sleeves. I have no intention of showing up at the Oscars dressed like a hooker."

Sam furrowed his brow. "Hookers don't wear Versace."

"And neither do I."

Sam looked at the dress and then looked back at her in absolute confusion. "I don't get it."

Delilah leaned forward. "I believe that what I wear is a reflection of my self-respect. I prefer to come across as a woman of dignity. 'Letting it all hang out' in a dress like that tells the world that my body is the best I have to offer. That's not true, and there is no point for me to misrepresent the woman I am and the values I stand for."

"But . . . it's Versace," Sam said again.

Delilah took a deep breath and gave up trying to explain her standards. "I have my own dress," she said calmly, although this was the first time she'd ever thought about the issue. She'd been counting on the fact that Sam wouldn't survive here for two weeks, meaning she wouldn't have to go to the Oscars at all.

Sam raised his eyebrows. "You do?"

"Yes, it's my prom dress from high school. My mom made it."

Sam's expression went flat. "What?"

"I said I'm wearing a dress my mom made."

"No way," he said with a shake of his head. "This is the Oscars. You don't show up in a homemade dress."

"I do."

He took some deep breaths. "Delilah, you just can't do that. This is far too important. Every woman there will be in designer gowns—gowns they've spent thousands of dollars on. That dress cost a fortune. You'll look radiant."

"I'll look radiant in my prom dress."

Sam actually stomped his foot, and she startled. "No, Delilah. I'm playing this your way. You can do something for me."

"No, Sam. This isn't up to you." His attitude was just making her that much more stubborn. She would not give in! "I don't wear sleeveless or backless—I'm a modest girl, and I'm not sidestepping my values for you or anyone else. The dress I'm going to wear is beautiful."

"It's . . . homemade!"

Delilah stood and signaled him to follow her. They went into her bedroom where she dug the plastic dress bag out of the back of her closet. She unzipped it and removed the dress, holding it up for him to see.

It was a lilac color with a flower pattern sown into the taffeta. The neck was high, almost oriental like, and it had pearl buttons across the shoulder. This was the dress she'd been wearing when Leif had officially asked her to wait for him. It was a dress she would always cherish.

Unfortunately, it wasn't quite as beautiful as she remembered it, especially when compared to the Versace gown in the study, but she lifted her chin and stood her ground. Maybe knowing this was what she was going to wear would have him packing his bags within the hour. She could only hope.

Sam stared at the dress for several seconds before turning to look at her. "Please tell me this is a sick joke. You can't possibly be planning to wear that. I'm begging you."

"And I'm still saying no."

Sam turned and left the room without saying another word. An hour later he tried to bring it up again. She was peeling potatoes for dinner, and she put up her hand and stopped him. "It's not a point worth discussing," Delilah said strongly. "Bring it up again and I'll have my mom sew a lace collar across the top."

Sam clenched his jaw and walked off. But he went outside, not to pack his bags. *Darn.* Delilah felt herself panic a little bit, too. If he really did make it the whole two weeks, she'd have to wear something to the Oscars. Did she really want to wear her prom dress from four years ago? Would it still fit? She certainly couldn't afford to buy a dress that would rival those worn by the other celebrities, and she sure wasn't going to let Sam pick out another one.

Maybe her mom could make some alterations and update the prom dress, or perhaps she could put another dress together.

While it was true she wouldn't wear the Versace, she didn't want to look like a fool either. She'd talk to her mom about it later.

For the next two days things continued in a similar pattern. Sam slept late both days and had to clean the floors by himself. But at least Delilah didn't have to supervise anymore. Neighbors had come over three times, and Sam and Delilah had had to stay out of sight. Luckily, they lived several miles out of town so drop-ins weren't common. Ironically, it was Delilah's supposed stay on the island that had people calling and stopping in to ask Mary how she was doing. The story was big news in town. Mary worked four days a week at the credit union and was constantly asked about her daughter when she went to work. She was considering taking some time off so she didn't have to lie to everyone. The lies were very hard for her.

Sam was sullen and pathetic, in Delilah's opinion. He tried to keep his complaints to himself, but it was nearly impossible for him to do so. He couldn't help but whine about the smell and the manure and the early mornings. Delilah would ignore it as long as she could and finally explode in a string of insults that would at least make him mad enough that he wouldn't talk anymore.

It was becoming a pattern Delilah didn't mind so much. She felt bad being mean, but he made it so easy. It was impossible not to treat him like an idiot when he tried so hard to be one. There was little doubt in her mind that his "ineptness" was feigned in hopes that it would get him out of work. She wondered how long it would take before he realized it wasn't working.

When Sam wasn't cleaning the barn he continued to flirt with Mary and tell her everything he'd ever seen Neil Diamond do. Delilah felt sure he made most of it up, but Mary didn't care. Delilah continued to roll her eyes at every opportunity— and re-teach Sam everything every day. He was like a sieve the way instructions seeped through him. The only times she caught a glimpse of the real Sam was when he thought she wasn't watching. When he had an audience, he acted as if this were an adventure. It was hard to believe that he wasn't having a great time. He deserved the Oscar if he could pull this off.

✳ Chapter Six ✳

On Thursday Sam woke up to the alarm he'd set for the first time the night before. He was tired of Delilah pounding on the door. Although he'd slept for eight hours, he felt as if he'd just laid down. Oh, he hated it here. But he didn't take too much time to wallow. He made it to the barn just a few minutes behind Delilah. He waited for her to say something positive about him getting up by himself, but she ignored him completely. *Typical.* Mary came into the milking barn around eight and said goodbye. She was going to Salt Lake for a few days to see her parents. Sam felt abandoned. Mary was the only person he felt understood him at all. As they returned to the chores at hand he caught a smug look on Delilah's face. He narrowed his eyes and dove into his tasks with greater fervor. Since the moment he'd gotten here she'd been pushing him to the limit—in every way. Not only was she snotty and rude, but she made it clear that she fully expected him to fail. He'd never met anyone like her in his life. She reminded him of his nemesis Carla Gooding in *Bad Moon Rising*. Carla Gooding was his boss in the movie, and she demanded perfection. Sam played Allen Red, and in the end he won Carla's heart. It was sure annoying how real life didn't parallel the movies as well as he hoped. But he was determined not to give in to the constant screaming in his head. He was Sam Hendricks—he could pull this off.

They finished the milking, and Sam and Delilah went into the house. Rhett went to take a shower before he left for Cedar City to meet with clients. Since his arrival, Sam had watched Mary and Delilah prepare the milk they used in their home. They would bring fresh milk in from the barn and pour it into shallow bowls and wait until the cream rose to the top. They would scrape the cream off the top and put the milk into a pitcher they kept in the fridge. Sam found it rather revolting.

He watched Delilah get the pitcher of milk out of the fridge and pour herself a bowl of cereal. When she was finished, she slid the cereal and the milk toward Sam. He regarded them with something less than excitement.

"I don't think I can ever drink milk again," he said.

Delilah shrugged her shoulders and took a big bite. Milk dribbled down her chin and Sam felt his stomach churn.

The process of getting milk from the stinky cows into a milk jug was too much information for Sam. Delilah said he'd get over it. He didn't believe her for a second and wondered if she hadn't slipped the cows a little something to make their smell that much more noxious while he was here.

"I was kind of hoping Mary left breakfast."

Delilah took another bite. "Nope, you're on your own."

Sam stood and opened the fridge. "There are no eggs?"

"Sure there are, but they're in the chicken coop. Mom usually gathers them. I guess she forgot."

Sam paused and tried to find the right way to ask who was going to get them. Finally she solved the quandary for him.

"If you want eggs, you'll have to get them yourself."

"Typical," Sam muttered as he let the fridge door swing shut. He turned and faced her, folding his arms across his chest and regarding her with irritation. The little role she was playing was getting really old.

"You really don't like me, do you?"

Delilah shrugged. "I don't know you," she said.

"As if you've tried very hard."

"I never try very hard to get to know the hired help," she said with a smile. "Besides, you're intent on 'acting' your part. It's not *you* that I see every day."

Sam smiled and nodded. "Would you rather I rant and rave and repeat how miserable it is here?"

Delilah raised her eyebrows. "Is it miserable?" She sounded too excited to hear it, and he made sure the vapor of honesty disappeared from his tone.

"It's not that bad," he said. "I mean, it's different from anything I've ever done, but I figure one day I'll get a role, and this will help me play it ever better. In *Ronny Coop* I went to a farm. The episode was about Ronny accidentally letting all the sheep loose. He had to figure out how to get them back in the pen. That farm was . . . different from this one, though." In the first place it was a set, not a farm, and the animals were either trained or tranquilized. Stuff was clean, and he was only there for a few hours.

Delilah leaned forward and clasped her hands together, resting her chin on them. "Everything's about playing parts for you, isn't it? I mean, your entire life is run by who you're pretending to be that day, that month, that year. I wonder if you don't ever get tired of it."

Sam smiled again and nodded. *Silly girl.* This conversation was finished. "Can you show me how to gather the eggs?"

Delilah stood up and put her bowl in the sink. "I'm not the one that wants eggs for breakfast. The coop is on the far side of the barn. The access door is painted pink. Unlatch it and lift it up to get in to the nesting boxes. The eggs will be in there, but be careful of the soft ones."

"Soft ones?"

"Sometimes the eggs don't harden, the shells stay soft. They feel like jelly, and they sometimes break all over you when you try to pick them up. If you leave them there the hens will eat them, and we'll get new eggs tomorrow."

Sam's stomach churned at the thought, but he forced a smile. He refused to give in to her attempts to scare him away from a chore that couldn't be that bad. Surely she was exaggerating.

Delilah was watching him intently. "You okay?"

"Fine," he said as offhandedly as he could manage.

"I'm going to take a shower. Make sure you latch the door when you finish."

Sam watched her disappear into her bedroom and shut the door, then looked around the room as his smile fell. Delilah had asked how long he thought he could keep up his act. With every passing day he was beginning to doubt his abilities more and more.

"I am Samuel Hendricks," he said to no one at all, trying

to remind himself. "I made sixteen million dollars on my last film. I have five people hired to answer my fan mail. I am a god among men . . . and I have to gather my own eggs. Wouldn't the American people love to know that?" Then he turned, grabbed his coat, and let himself out into the frigid morning.

Sam found the chicken coop easily enough. It was made entirely out of old doors of various colors. Some were right side up, some were sideways or cut in half. Together they made a big, ugly box. One end of the box had about twenty square feet of fenced area where a few of the bravest chickens were strutting and scratching. The other end had one door set up on hinges the normal way. He figured the door was in case someone wanted to go inside the coop—though he couldn't figure out what could possibly possess anyone to do that. He thought the cows had smelled bad. This new smell was horrid.

Next to the door that led inside the coop was a bright pink, horizontal door. He had to survey it for a minute to see how it worked. It had hinges at the top, so it opened like a car trunk. It was also very light-weight and fastened down by several latches. Once the latches were undone he lifted the door and had access to several boxes with straw in them. The eggs were there waiting for him. But he couldn't bring himself to touch them.

Sam wasn't as big an idiot as Delilah thought he was. He knew how to cook . . . a little. And in his vast culinary experience he knew that eggs were supposed to be white. These eggs were various shades of brown and they had . . . gunk . . . on the discolored shells. Straw and feathers added further decoration, and he couldn't force himself to ignore how unclean they were. To think he'd ever eaten these alien things was frightening. To even consider cooking them himself, on purpose, was impossible. He let the door shut without touching a single egg. Shaking his head in disgust he walked back to the house and wondered what cereal tasted like with water instead of milk.

Cody watched the taped replay of the morning kitchen scene and couldn't help but laugh out loud. Up until this, all they had gotten were the charming dinners and Delilah's snotty comments. Cody had hoped to see some of Sam winning Delilah over, but he was beginning to doubt that it could happen at all. She seemed totally uninterested, even bored with the acclaimed actor. But Cody could use that spin, too. That's what he was, after all—a spin doctor. It was his personal duty to make sure everyone knew who Sam Hendricks was. Delilah's less than positive comments were proof in and of themselves of how important a job he had. The battle over whether or not to use this stuff was still going on inside him. Sam's blatant "no" continued to ring in his ears each time he thought what the best use of this film would be. He'd considered making a kind of reality TV documentary, but he'd need permission from the Glenshaws to use it as a TV special or anything like that, and he doubted that would happen. The only real choice would be to "leak" the tapes to the tabloid shows. The Glenshaws would flip, but Sam could smooth it over. However, that brought him back to the problem of Sam himself. He was adamant about not using any of this, despite its entertainment appeal. Maybe Cody could convince him otherwise . . . but what if he couldn't? *Well, it's something to think about,* Cody thought as he got up and headed out to the pool. The best part of this whole thing was that he had free reign of the house and didn't have to play babysitter. He liked that a lot. Almost too much. Maybe when Sam came back he'd ask for a place of his own. It had been a year of twenty-four-hour supervision. Surely Cody had earned the right to get a small portion of his own life back again. Despite Sam's belief to the contrary, there was more to life than Sam Hendricks.

✯✯✯

After the morning milking the next day, Sam and Delilah came inside and collapsed in the kitchen chairs. Sam would do anything for a cup of coffee. He wished Delilah were a little more materialistic, but since she wasn't, he had nothing to bribe her with that would relax her piousness about the coffee. Resting his elbows on the table, he dropped his face into his hands as Delilah opened the fridge.

"Where are the eggs?" she asked.

"If you want eggs, get them yourself," he responded. "I heard that somewhere recently."

She turned to look at him, tilting her head to one side. "Didn't you get them yesterday? There should be plenty left over."

"Obviously not," Sam said. "It grossed me out."

Delilah groaned and shifted her weight. Her blue eyes narrowed, and she folded her arms across her chest. "Great," she said. "Now they'll be frozen, which means they'll go in the trash. Good going."

Sam felt his irritation grow. "You didn't tell me I *had* to get them, just if I wanted some. Once I saw what they looked like I decided I don't eat eggs anymore."

"If I'd known you hadn't gotten them, I'd have collected them myself. Now they all go to waste because you're such a baby."

"You should have told me it was important."

"You should have known."

"Well, I didn't!"

"What else is new?" she yelled back as she slammed the fridge and walked toward the back door. As soon as he heard the back door shut, Sam swore up a storm, laying out in colorful detail just what he thought of Delilah, her chickens, and her blasted eggs. Less than a minute later the door burst open again.

"You didn't latch the door!" Delilah screamed as soon as she entered.

Sam spun around in his seat, ready for a fight. "What latch?"

"On the box door!" Delilah's nostrils flared, and he realized she was really mad.

That just made him more angry. "Box door?" he asked. "I don't know what you're talking about."

"The sideways door that opens into the laying boxes—you didn't latch it."

"Sure I did," he said, but he could sense his own hesitation. Did he latch it? He couldn't remember.

"The latch keeps the raccoons out. If it isn't latched, they can get in."

"A raccoon couldn't open that door," he said with a shake of his head. "I could barely figure it out."

"That doesn't say much about your intelligence, does it! They can open the door—hence half a dozen latches to make sure they don't."

"And so what? They get in and eat some frozen eggs I didn't gather. It saves having to throw them out."

Delilah took a deep breath. "They didn't eat the eggs, you moron!" she screamed. "They ate the chickens!"

A heavy silence filled the room, and Sam's anger drained away as Delilah glared at him, her eyes narrowed and her face red. "What?" he asked.

"Chicken parts are all over the place."

Sam started feeling small. "They ate all of them?"

"There are a few left," she spat, her eyes still blazing. "But most of them are dead. I can't believe you're such an idiot."

"You didn't tell me to latch it," Sam countered.

"Yes, I did—don't try and make this my fault. Take some responsibility, Sam! Your irresponsible behavior just wiped out our entire flock."

"They're chickens," Sam said in sharp tones. He'd never in his life been talked to the way she was insulting him, and he couldn't take much more of it. "Chill out."

"It takes six months for chicks to lay, and then it's a few months before they produce regularly. To you they're chickens, but we trade them for all kinds of things. For us they're pot roasts, haircuts, food. But I don't know why I'm even expecting you to get it. You don't get any of this." She turned to leave just as Rhett walked in. She quickly took the opportunity to explain to her father what had happened.

"Is this true?" Rhett asked once she finished. He looked at Sam with eyes that seemed to look right through him. His calm and non-judgmental attitude brought on Sam's first feelings of guilt.

For several seconds Sam waged an internal battle with himself. This whole thing was ridiculous. He could buy them a million chickens to replace them. At the same time he was embarrassed to have made such a stupid mistake. The way Rhett was looking at him made his justifications particularly lacking. He looked down at the floor and shrugged. "I don't know . . . maybe . . . well, probably." He looked up and met the other man's eyes, ignoring Delilah's glaring expression. "I'm sorry, Rhett. I didn't mean to leave it open. I didn't think about it."

Rhett nodded. "You can make it right by cleaning up the mess."

Sam grimaced, but it was hard to complain when Rhett was being so mild and even about the whole thing. Delilah nodded in agreement.

"Delilah will help you," Rhett added as an afterthought.

"What?" she countered, turning to look at her father with horror.

"Did you show him how to latch up the coop and explain how important it was?"

"Any idiot would know how to latch the door."

"Delilah Anne," Rhett said with a warning tone.

She pursed her lips and looked away. "No, I didn't show him, but I did tell him."

"Then you have fault, too. I'll fix up some biscuits and gravy while you two clean up the mess. Throw the carcasses in the oil can and put the lid on it. We'll burn them later."

Delilah didn't talk to Sam as they scoured the coop and yard for chicken parts, frozen thanks to the cold. Sam nearly lost his lunch several times and scratched "chicken" off of his list of foods he could still eat. At this rate he'd be a vegan by the time he left. It turned out that six of the twenty-one chickens had survived the assault, but they were agitated and high-strung.

They would run and screech whenever Sam or Delilah got too close to them. The smell of blood and meat added sickening warmth to the winter air, and made it that much harder not to throw up.

As they went about their grisly chore, Sam was amazed at how casual Delilah was about it. Sure, she was mad and muttering under her breath, but the women he'd known in the past threw fits over steaks not cooked right or if the potatoes touched the fish on their plates. He couldn't imagine any of them picking up severed chicken heads. He couldn't believe *he* was doing it.

When they finally finished dumping the remains in the oil barrel, Sam grabbed the sleeve of her coat to keep her from walking away. She turned to face him, still regarding him with contempt. "I'm sorry," he said, and was surprised to realize that he meant it. "It was my fault, and you shouldn't have had to do this."

For a moment she seemed to be considering an angry retort, but she apparently thought better of it. Maybe sharing something this unique was what they had needed this whole time. "I should have shown you what to do," she said. It was a forced apology, and he doubted her heart was in it. But he was used to insincerity so he didn't mind.

They held one another's eyes for just a moment before she turned and began walking again. It wasn't much of a reconciliation but he felt lifted by it.

They were still several yards from the house when the sound of a car coming up the drive froze them mid-step. They looked at each other for just an instant before they ran. Moments later, flattened against the side of the house, they listened as a car door opened and shut. Then they heard the back door open and shut as well.

"Doyle!" they heard Rhett call out. "What brings you here?" He seemed to be speaking loudly, probably to make sure they heard the discussion.

Doyle replied with a muffled response they couldn't make out. For nearly a minute Sam and Delilah stood there in silence as the voices droned on.

"You guys sure get a lot of visitors," Sam finally whispered.

"We're so out of the way out here that not many people bother coming over—thanks to you that's different now."

Sam turned his head and looked at her. "I'm sure tired of everything being my fault."

Delilah let out an exaggerated sigh. "Me too," she said. But she turned her head and smiled. "Sorry—I'll try to be nice."

"I'm not convinced you know how," Sam replied. Her mouth turned up into a little smile that told him she'd actually listened to what he'd said. They were silent for several more seconds. The voices around the side of the house continued.

"How long are they going to talk out there?" he muttered under his breath. They'd been outside for over half an hour. The moisture was starting to seep through his Nike sneakers. He looked down at them and cringed. They were nearly new when he got here. Now they were brown and smelly. Rhett had offered him an old pair of his son's boots, but Sam refused. Someone else had worn them, and he wasn't about to inherit their foot diseases. He had limits. But he was wondering if he ought to renegotiate those limits with himself. The Nikes weren't made for this kind of thing.

"Doyle can talk for hours," Delilah said. She reached over and tugged on Sam's sleeve. "Come on, let's see if we can sneak into the house."

Sam followed her around to the back of the house that faced the acreage where they grew their hay in the summer. The farm house was old, with wood siding and small windows that were located high on the walls. He and Delilah stood underneath one of them and surveyed it. It was at least seven feet up on the wall. "Surely there are windows closer to the ground."

"Yes, there are," she agreed, putting her hands in the back pockets of her jeans and rocking back on her heels. Her hair was down, and a red knit cap was pulled down over her ears. When she spoke, her breath made little clouds in the air around her face. "But the bathroom window is the only one that doesn't lock."

"Typical," Sam said. He should be used to things being as difficult as possible around here, but it still surprised him. "When I played Johnny Free in *Lawless Lovers*, he used to sneak into his ex-wife's house through a window, but it was at ground level."

Delilah laughed and he looked at her, not sure what was so funny.

"Well, isn't Johnny the lucky one," she said as she stopped laughing. "Here's the catch with *our* window, however. You have to jimmy the window to get it to slide open—and we can't do it standing here."

"So what do you suggest?"

She turned to look at him. "I need a boost." She lifted up one foot indicating for him to hold it.

He grimaced and looked at her. "Do you know where that shoe has been?"

She laughed again, and he realized what a nice sound it was. He liked knowing she found him amusing, even if she did think he was a moron—it was progress nonetheless. "Put on your work gloves, then," she said.

Good idea, he thought to himself as he dug the gloves out of his back pockets. Once his hands were safely ensconced in their leather protectors, he laced his fingers together and leaned over so that she could put her foot into the stirrup he'd created. He grunted when she hoisted herself up and then wobbled back and forth trying to balance her weight.

"Stop moving," she said as she grabbed onto his neck to keep from falling. His face went directly into her coat as he continued to step back and forth. "Sam, stop it."

He tried to say, "I'm trying," but with his face against her coat it came out mumbled. He felt her lean to the side, and he moved with her until his shoulder slammed against the side of the house. At least he could use it for support now. It seemed to take forever before she finally jumped down out of his hands. He was panting for breath, and she put a hand over her mouth to keep from laughing.

"You're heavy," he finally said. He stood up straighter in

hopes of recovering some dignity. It didn't seem to help. She was still laughing.

"I hope we're not going to discuss my weight again," she finally said.

"It's off limits, remember?" he said. He stretched out his arms and hoped he hadn't torn anything.

She indicated for him to put his hands out again. "I got it open. Now, just lift me up to the window, and I should be able to slide in." He took a deep breath and laced his fingers again. As she rose up she said, "You know I'm only a size twelve and I'm five foot eight—it's not like I have a weight problem."

"We don't discuss your weight," Sam heaved.

She put her hands on the sill of the window and hoisted herself up onto it, supporting herself with her arms. She looked over her shoulder. "You're used to anorexic stick women—real women have a shape to them."

"Yes, I know," he said, and then just to make her mad he gave her body a long perusing look.

"Very funny," she said as she pulled herself through the window. A few seconds later she stuck her head out. "I don't know if I'm going to let you in after that."

"You brought it up," he said with a shrug of his shoulders. He could tell by the look on her face that she wasn't that offended. She leaned farther out and held out her hands. Sam removed his gloves and took hold as she pulled him up. By using the side of the house he was able to take a few steps up the wall toward the window, but he seriously doubted she could pull him up all the way. Things like this required stunt doubles.

"What are you doing?"

Delilah and Sam startled and turned their heads to see Rhett standing there, watching them with an odd look on his face. Sam's foot slipped off the side of the house. Delilah pulled on his hand, but it was too late. His hands slipped out of her grip, and he landed on his behind in a rather mushy and very cold spot of grass.

"Are you okay?" she called out.

Sam cursed in his mind and stood up, twisting around to

see that his entire backside was covered in wet sludge. He looked up at her. "I'm great," he said flatly. Then he looked at Rhett. "You're guest is gone?"

"He's been gone for awhile. I knew if I kept him talking outside he wouldn't stay for long. I've been looking for you guys, and I guess I got here just in time." He clapped Sam on the back and headed for the house with a big grin on his face.

Delilah was still in the window trying not to laugh. "Sorry," she said. "I guess we should have waited a little longer."

"Yeah, I guess so." He pointed in Rhett's direction. "I think I'll use the door if you don't mind."

She rested her elbows on the sill and put her chin in her hands. She gave him a pouty look. "Awe, you're no fun," she said. Then she brightened. "First one to the bathroom gets the first shower."

"You're already in the bathroom," he said.

"Oh, you're right," she said with a grin. "Lucky me!" With that she snapped the window closed. Sam shook his head and walked toward the back door. The wetness had soaked into his skin, and he was uncomfortable. But the experience hadn't been a total loss. At least he knew there was more to Delilah than snotty comments. Who knew?

To Sam's dismay, Rhett could only cook one meal: biscuits and gravy. Mary couldn't stand it, so he was only allowed to cook it when she was out of town. They had it for breakfast, lunch, and dinner the first two days, and Sam began to understand Mary's disdain. Delilah, however, seemed to like it as much as Rhett did. On the third day they ran out of sausage. Sam breathed a sigh of relief when Delilah announced that she would make dinner. He had been hoping for something a little better than grilled cheese sandwiches, but Delilah said she was too tired to cook. They were just finishing dinner Friday night when they heard the back door open. All three of them looked up as Mary entered the room.

Hellos and hugs were exchanged. Sam felt his spirits raise just knowing she was back. Rhett lifted his face to give his wife a welcome-home kiss as she passed by. Delilah sat back down and immediately asked how the trip was in between drinks of milk.

"It was fine. Grandma and Grandpa are doing okay. Mom's having a hard time doing her crochet, what with the cold weather, but that's to be expected." She turned to look at Delilah. "I brought you something, though."

Delilah lifted her eyebrows. "A present?"

"Just a little something I found in town." She looked past Delilah's head and everyone followed her gaze. Delilah swiveled in her chair. A man stepped out from the shadows of the hallway. He about six feet tall and although he wasn't slender, he wasn't thick either. But he looked solid, like a man who made good use of everything he'd been given. He had bright blue eyes and short brown hair that already showed a receding hairline he would mourn in a few years. His ears stuck out a little too far from his head, but it seemed to fit him. He was dressed in wrangler jeans, leather work boots, and a sweatshirt that boasted a logo for "Lucky Jeans." In his hand was a baseball cap. He looked like the kind of guy Sam would expect to see on the farm, and he wondered if this guy wasn't another worker. Sam liked that idea.

"Hey, Dee."

Delilah had been frozen until he spoke. In the next instant she rocketed from her chair and shrieked as she flew across the room. "Leif!" She threw herself into his arms and held on tight. He wrapped his arms around her and the two of them rocked gently from side to side. *Not a worker I guess*, Sam thought to himself. *This must be the fiancé.* The merest tremble of jealousy tried to tempt him. He refused to give in. Even with her renewed attempts at being nice, Delilah was still insufferable. He wasn't the least bit in want of her attentions.

But it bothered him none the less. He wasn't used to being the man without female attention, and he didn't like losing at anything. Mary and Rhett shared an indulgent smile, and Sam felt another kind of jealousy. Being with this family had shown him a lot of things he'd never seen before—Rhett talking to Delilah as if they were equals, family dinners, and these weird prayers at every meal and before bed. It was odd and uncomfortable, yet it touched him, too. He tried to remember if he'd ever sat down to dinner with either of his parents and a woman he was interested in. After a moment he decided it had never happened and it probably never would. He didn't date the kind of women one might bring home, nor did his parents have that kind of interest in his life.

"When did you get home?" Delilah asked as she pulled back. "I thought you had another week to go." Her face was vibrant and Sam had never seen her smile so wide. She didn't let go of Leif, either. Instead she kept her arms around his neck and played with the hair at the nape of his neck.

"Yeah, well, something was wrong with the last delivery and so they cut the trip short. I just pulled into town about an hour ago. Your mom saw my truck at the yard and asked if I wanted a ride out here. She was good enough to wait while I finished up. I guess she was right that you would be excited to see me."

"Are you kidding?" Delilah laughed. "I've been counting the hours. Are you staying?"

"Mary said you could use the help since you can't very well bring extra workers on and have them realize you're here. I'll go home at night, but I won't have another route till next week. So I'm all yours during the day."

Delilah squeezed him again. "I'm so glad," she said as she pulled back once more. "I wish I'd fixed something better for dinner."

Sam took a bite of his sandwich and looked away. *I thought she was too tired*, he thought to himself. She'd cook for Leif but not for him. Hmph.

"Don't worry about that," Leif said. Delilah turned back toward the table but didn't let go of Leif's hand. As she turned, Leif looked at Sam for just the briefest of moments. Sam felt challenged by the look. That lifted his spirits somewhat; Leif thought he was competition. It was about time someone gave him the respect he deserved!

Leif ate a sandwich, and then Mary offered to whip up a dessert while the rest of them went out for the evening milking. When Sam took his dish to the sink he put his arm around Mary and gave her a squeeze, wanting to ensure he stayed in her good graces. "I'm so glad you're home," he said. She blushed, and he kissed her on the cheek. As he pulled back he whispered, "Don't ever leave me again."

She blushed even deeper and shooed him away. It was nice to know his charm hadn't deserted him completely.

✭ Chapter Seven ✭

Rhett went in when Miguel and Eric left that night. The final chores were left up to Leif, Delilah, and Sam. Delilah and Leif seemed unable to be more than five feet apart, and they did their chores together. Sam tried to stay out of their way. Every time one of them laughed, his jaw would tense. After an hour his whole face ached. Living on the fringes of their puppy love was worse than cleaning up mangled chickens.

They finally finished and headed back to the house. Sam was inside less than three seconds when he heard something that made him freeze in his tracks. Challenging the speed of light, he kicked off his shoes, threw his coat against the wall, and followed the sound. When he reached the doorway of Rhett's study, he froze again. His mouth hung open and his eyes grew wide. There on Rhett's desk was a computer monitor displaying the Lakers game. The sound of the crowd seemed to be in tune with his own heartbeat. A warmth overcame him, and he knew beyond a doubt that he hadn't felt this happy since he'd come here.

Rhett looked up in surprise. "You a Lakers fan or a Sonics fan?"

Sam walked into the room with his gaze fixed on the screen. "Lakers," he answered. "Delilah said you didn't have TV." Karl Malone blocked a shot and passed to Shaq. Sam's eyes darted back and forth, absorbing every movement of the ball.

"We don't, but there's nothing worth watching other than sports anyway. I signed up for one of these Internet subscriptions that allows me to watch the games in real time."

Sam sank into a chair and looked at his benefactor. "Thank you," he breathed. Then he looked back at the screen and forgot all about cows and chickens for the next hour and a half. It was the first time he hadn't felt as if he were on another planet—it was a magical moment. If there was basketball, there was hope.

The next morning they did the milking—again. Sam wondered how on earth anyone could live their life knowing they had to milk cows at five o'clock every single morning. The only thing that made it bearable was knowing he only had seven of these mornings to go. When he'd played a serial killer in *All for One* he'd had to be covered head to toe in mud for seven days straight. The only way he'd made it through was by promising himself a reward once it was done. It was after that portion of shooting that he'd bought the apartment in Manhattan.

For the rest of the day, he was committed to figuring out what he would give himself once this was behind him. It was harder than it seemed. There were few things he could dream up that would make this worthwhile.

After the milking, Sam made himself a peanut butter and jam sandwich, which was becoming a staple of his diet since couldn't eat milk, eggs, or chicken anymore. It was only to fend off death by dehydration that he could stand drinking the tap water and preferred it when Mary mixed it with Kool-Aid—at least it didn't taste like sand that way. As he was finishing his sandwich, Rhett announced they were going to fix some fences. Sam had been hoping to take a shower, but Delilah and Leif jumped on a four-wheeler together and took off for the back pastures before he had a chance to attempt a protest. Sam stayed with Rhett and gathered shovels and work gloves. There were two four-wheelers left, so Sam could have his own. Rhett gave him a crash course in driving. It wasn't as easy as it looked, and while trying to back up, Sam knocked over the barrel—now full of chicken parts that hadn't yet been burned. The lid bounced off when it hit the ground and chicken remains spilled all over the place. Sam cursed, and Rhett reminded him that those words weren't allowed on the farm.

Sam didn't know how they survived without swearing.

It took a few minutes to pick up the mangled poultry, and then Sam concentrated even harder on his driving lessons. After a few more minutes they were finally on their way to meet up with Delilah and Leif.

Rhett was in the lead, and Sam followed him closely. Delilah and Leif sat on their shared four-wheeler facing one another and wrapped together like a ball of aluminum foil. Sam rolled his eyes, just as Delilah would have. It was getting old. For the next five hours they re-dug post holes, strung barbed wire, and mended existing fence lines. Sam's fingers were throbbing from trying to manipulate the thick wire, and he nearly shouted "Yehaw" when Rhett announced they were done for the day. Sam's entire face was frozen. He couldn't feel his feet, and he was the first one back to the house. *Thank goodness that's over*, he thought as he plopped down on a kitchen chair and thanked Mary for the hot cocoa she put in front of him. The other three came in soon after.

"How did it go?" Mary asked as she handed them their mugs.

"Pretty well," Rhett answered. "We won't work tomorrow, it being the Sabbath, but by Tuesday we should have it done."

Sam froze mid-sip and cursed loudly in his mind. *There's more?* He was beginning to think there was no reward on this entire planet that was going to be worth this.

"That's wonderful," Mary said as she turned back to the sink. Then she turned to face them again. "Oh, I meant to ask you. What happened to the chickens?"

Sam groaned and stood. "I'm going to take a shower," he announced. He had no desire to hear the saga related again.

Under the hot water he remembered all the lousy experiences he'd had in his life. Most of them had to do with roles he had played, so it was nearly impossible to compare them to this, where he wasn't even getting paid. He'd thought things were looking up after he and Delilah cleaned up the mutilated chickens. She'd been much nicer, and they'd even had a few nearly decent conversations. There had been definite progress made between the two of them. And then Leif showed up.

There was no room in her starry eyes for Sam anymore. She revolved around Leif like a planet around the sun. It was very annoying. *He* was Sam Hendricks, a millionaire sex symbol. Leif was a truck driver, for heaven's sake. It made no sense. In fact, he wasn't all that sure what it was he liked about Delilah. She wasn't like any other woman he'd known—maybe that was it. Maybe it was the sheer oddity of her that made her so interesting. But with Leif here it didn't matter. She had eyes only for him.

Forcing himself to change his own train of thought, he focused on how grateful he was that no one would know he was here. *Thank goodness.* He couldn't think of anything more embarrassing than having all of America know he was a farmhand—and an accessory to a chicken massacre—that couldn't win the girl. At that moment he resolved never to tell a single soul how he'd spent these two weeks—not that he'd ever intended to. But there had always been a small possibility of talking about it one day down the road. That possibility no longer existed. He'd never felt so inept and uncoordinated as he had this last week. No one but the Glenshaws would ever know.

When he came out from taking his shower, the conversation on chickens had run its course. Rhett and Mary were elsewhere, but the way Delilah and Leif stopped talking when he walked into the kitchen let him know he was the topic of discussion. He liked being the center of attention though, so he wasn't bothered by their gossip.

"Don't stop because of me," he said with a smile. "I'm my favorite topic of conversation."

Leif smiled and Delilah shook her head. "I was just telling Leif what happened with the press conference—he never saw it."

Sam nodded and Delilah continued, explaining how Cody had arranged for her body double to go to this fancy-shmancy resort.

"So who is this Cody guy?" Leif asked.

Sam grabbed a brownie from the plate on the table. That

was one thing he really liked about being here—continual baked goods. "He's my personal assistant—business manager—publi-cist; a little of everything."

"So what does he do?" Leif continued.

"Pretty much anything Sam doesn't want to do, I think," Delilah cut in. "The times I've been around them, Cody softens Sam's stupid comments, arranges everything, carries the bags—he's like a built-in babysitter."

"He's not my babysitter," Sam said with a shake of his head. He'd heard his assistants referred to that way before, and it really bothered him. "Mostly Cody's supposed to schedule appointments and interviews for me. But he also does a lot of the behind-the-scenes things—and well, he does do pretty much anything I ask him to do. It's a great situation. I highly recommend it." He popped the rest of the brownie into his mouth and eyed another one. To keep his body in perfect shape he avoided sugar most of the time. But with all the work they were doing he had little doubt he could find a way to burn off the extra calories. He grabbed another one.

"A paid brown-noser," Leif said thoughtfully. "Nah, I think it would drive me crazy. I'd feel too bad asking someone to do all the grunge work for me."

"No offense, but I think my grunge work is a lot different than yours. Cody has a pretty sweet situation, if you ask me. I pay him through the nose to make my life easier. And I'm his ticket to Hollywood hobnobbing. Without me, he wouldn't have half the lifestyle he's got. He loves every minute of it."

Delilah snorted and stood up, taking her plate to the sink. "If you ask me, he's *your* ticket to Hollywood hobnobbing. He's the brains of this outfit."

Sam shook his head with disgust. "Hardly," he said. "There are two kinds of people in Hollywood—actors and wannabes. Cody is a dyed-in-the-wool wannabe. By working for me he gets paid to live like I do. For an average guy that couldn't get an acting job if his life depended on it, he's got it good."

"You talk about him like he's a pet," Delilah said. She turned on the water and started rinsing dishes.

"Here, Cody," Sam said as if he were calling a dog. "Here, Cody-Cody-Cody."

"You are horrible," Delilah said as she turned to face him.

She wasn't laughing, and Sam was surprised. "It was a joke," he explained. He looked to Leif for support.

"You're on your own, man," Leif said as he bit into a brownie.

Delilah turned back to the sink and continued, "He's a person, Sam. A man with goals and feelings. What would he think if he'd heard what you just said?"

"Oh, lighten up," Sam said with irritation. *It was a joke, a funny one. Why was she so judgmental?* "Cody would know it was a joke . . . and he wouldn't freak because he wouldn't want to give up his free ride."

"I wouldn't be so sure," Leif said as he stood and stretched his arms. "People can only take so much. Sooner or later he might just surprise you."

"I doubt it," Sam said, tiring of this discussion. They obviously didn't understand how the Hollywood hierarchy worked. "And even if he did, big deal. I'd have a new assistant by the end of the day, and Cody would be kicked to the curb. That's how it works."

"One more reason for me to hate Hollywood," Delilah commented.

Sam shook his head and stood up. "If you don't like my answers, then don't ask me what I think."

Delilah turned and snapped her fingers. "Now that's a brilliant idea."

⭐⭐⭐

Cody usually watched the tapes with complete amusement. He loved watching Delilah's snide comments and Sam's inability to counter them. It was perhaps the first time in Sam's life that he'd had to take that kind of abuse, and it was entertaining to watch him deal with it. Until now. When this sequence of filming was finished he rewound it and watched it again.

Then he went for a long walk on the beach—Sam's beach.

Cody was an objective man, and knew that in Sam's eyes what he'd said was funny—a simple joke. He didn't think that being Cody's "ticket to Hollywood hobnobbing" was at all demeaning. Sam truly believed that being his lapdog was Cody's life-long dream. The more Cody replayed what had been said on that tape, the smaller he felt. The smaller he felt, the angrier he got.

Cody found himself remembering the middle-of-the-night phone calls demanding that he go buy a particular brand of ice cream that took trips to four stores to locate. Or the time Sam had Cody distract one girlfriend while the other one finished breakfast in the next room. There had been last-minute travel plans to check out a new club that messed up weeks of sched-uled appearances. Cody had been dragged from AA meeting to AA meeting, and then from bar to bar. Having these last seven days to himself, to set his own schedule and make his own choices, was the perfect soil in which to grow the discontent-ment Sam sowed with his comments to Delilah and Leif. "Here, Cody," reverberated in his brain. "Here, Cody-Cody-Cody." It made him boil inside.

Several months ago, Cody had been offered a personal assistant position with a man by the name of Barry Bradshaw. Barry had played many minor roles, but had yet to make it big. They met at one of Sam's parties and hit it off. Barry was orig-inally from Denver, Cody's hometown, and they had a lot in common. A few weeks later Cody had received a phone call from Barry. The job offer included a house and a car of his own. At the time of Barry's offer, Cody hadn't really consid-ered it. Sam was at the top of his game, and Cody knew it was because of his efforts that Sam continued to do so well. None of Sam's assistants had been as good as Cody was, not even close. Leaving his prodigy to flounder at that point was unthinkable. Barry had said if Cody ever changed his mind to give him a call. Cody hadn't thought much about the standing offer. But now . . . his loyalty to Sam was faltering. And if he was going to leave this behind, there was no better way than to go out with a "bang" that would shake Sam to his very core. Sam said Cody did whatever Sam told him to do, that he hadn't the intelligence to do much without him—well, he'd see just how smart Cody really was. In fact, the world would see it.

Cody called Barry and asked if the offer still stood. Barry didn't hesitate to say that it did. In fact, he would fire his currant assistant that day if Cody was willing to sign a contract. Cody had a few questions first. They spoke for nearly an hour about the specifics. It wasn't a "be at my beck and call" kind of job. Instead, Cody would be in charge of appearances, articles, and managing the press. He would accompany Barry to interviews and events, but when Barry wasn't involved in the spotlight, Cody was free to manage his time how ever he'd like. Barry had a new wife, and he planned on having plenty of free time to spend with her. His free time would be nearly equal to Cody's free time, and Cody would be given a house Barry owned in Palm Springs. After watching the tape again, Cody took a long soak in Sam's hot tub and fantasized about his new house. By the end of the day, he'd made up his mind, and "Operation Snoopy" turned sinister.

✸ Chapter Eight ✸

After three more days, Sam could hardly move. They had taken it easy on Sunday, but starting Monday morning things had turned sour—fast. Sam was so tired and sore he wasn't sure he could get out of bed. A very small part of him had been glad to have Leif in the beginning. He had assumed that the extra help would make the work load lighter. Whatever! Leif was a "can do anything" kind of guy. With his continued presence, Rhett pulled out the big guns of farm chores. In addition to the daily milking, cleaning the barn, rotating the straw, and orchestrating the feed, they had spent the last two days mending fences, cleaning the sheds, and doing other odds and ends. Where Sam had had a couple of hours every day to wallow in self-pity or take a nap, those hours were now filled with a hundred other things to do.

Sam was getting fed up and wondered when these people ever took a break. At the same time, they had this perpetual satisfaction with their lives that confused him. How could they be so happy when they had to work so hard? It was sheer will power and a competitive streak that kept him here at all. It had been ten days, and knowing he had four days to go was overwhelming. However, the thought of giving up was incomprehensible. He was Sam Hendricks. He could do anything—everybody said so. He wished he wasn't beginning to doubt them.

It was a particularly cold morning Wednesday, and Sam pulled his jacket even tighter around him as he headed to the barn. Leif and Delilah walked hand in hand ahead of him, and he watched their companionship with annoyance. Sure, they enjoyed each other's company and were from the same world, but what did Leif really have to offer? He wasn't that good-looking, and he drove a truck for a living. Sam couldn't figure out what it was about him that warranted the admiration and affection that Delilah oozed all over him. Instead of getting used to it, Sam found himself more and more annoyed by it every day. Leif slept at his house in town, but he was here in the mornings before Sam got up, and Delilah walked him out to his car after the chores were done every night. It was pretty much the same as him living here and it was getting more irritating every day.

They finished the morning milking around nine o'clock and headed back to the house for breakfast before they had to go work on fences again. Sam had never seen so many pathetic fences, and he hated them. His hands were all cut up, thanks to the barbed wires, and his arms and back were stiff. He'd give his Oscar nomination for a Jacuzzi and a tall beer.

Eating his breakfast as slowly as possible helped put off the inevitable, but eventually he ran out of food. Grumbling, he got up from the table and put his work boots back on while Leif and Delilah discussed who would and would not be a bridesmaid at the wedding. It was as if he didn't exist anymore. A few yards away from the house, Leif squeezed Delilah's hand and pulled her to him for a quick kiss before heading left—away from the four wheelers they would take to the awaiting fences.

"Where are you going?" Sam hollered. Leif sure as heck better not be getting out of the fence repair. If anyone deserved a day off it was Sam.

Leif turned. "I'm going to start working on some new shelves in the shed now that it's cleaned up."

"You're not helping with the fences?"

"I think you guys can handle it." He looked over at Delilah and shared a smile that seemed to communicate some kind of silent joke they shared. Sam had no doubt who the butt of that joke was. Leif looked back at Sam. "You can help me if you'd rather." Sam detected a definite challenge in the offer—as if building shelves required some skill he didn't possess.

Was he kidding? Anything was better than repairing fences. But he played it down. "Sure, if you need my help."

Once in the shed, Leif began explaining what they were

going to do. He talked about support beams, measurements, tools—Sam only half-listened. He was just glad he wasn't in the pasture. All the lingo was French to him anyway.

"So what do you want me to do?" Sam asked once Leif stopped playing Bob Vila.

"Help me bring in the two-by-fours Rhett picked up in town yesterday. We'll go from there."

It wasn't a bad job, Sam decided after twenty minutes. There was a space heater that kept the shed warm, and Leif was a good teacher—a lot like Rhett. Leif measured out the wood, and Sam got to play with the saw. He messed up now and then, but there was plenty of wood so it worked out okay. After a while, Leif decided Sam should measure and he should cut. But Sam didn't like that, and Leif eventually decided to go back to measuring the wood himself when Sam messed up six measurements in a row. Then Sam got to play with the saw again. He liked that better. The smell of fresh cut wood seemed to awaken a part of himself he'd never known existed, and he decided to have a woodshop built at his Malibu house. Maybe he'd take up carpentry as a hobby. His fans would love it. He could auction off furniture he made on eBay. It would get great press.

As they worked, Sam kept waiting for Leif to tell him what a quick study he was, but Leif seemed to be holding back. He was probably intimidated, not only by Sam's good looks, but by the speed in which he was picking up this new skill.

"So how long have you and Delilah known each other?" Sam asked an hour or so into the project.

"Most of our lives," Leif answered as he re-measured a piece of wood Sam had just cut and tossed it into the ever-growing reject pile. Sam thought he was being a little over discriminating—what was the big deal about being a couple of inches off? "I was born in Big Fork, and Delilah moved here when we were both six. We've been in the same ward and schools ever since."

"Ward?" Sam asked. "What kind of ward?" Several possibilities came to mind. Maternity ward, cancer ward, but first and most likely was the mental ward. That would explain a lot.

"Ward is what we call the congregation of our church."

Oh good, Mormon stuff. Sam had been avoiding any and all talk of religion. He wasn't about to get into it now. He didn't comment, and so Leif continued. "We've been in the same classes at school and then we served in the student council together. I was president, she was vice president. That's when we started dating. We've been together ever since."

"Sounds like you were meant to be together," Sam said, but he turned away and rolled his eyes. Someone pass the salt. He was about to keel over from sugar shock.

"It sure seems that way," Leif continued. "I went on my mission while she went to college for a year. When I got back after two years, I started this truck training while she was finishing up her nanny job in New York. We're getting married in May."

In the milk barn, no doubt, Sam thought to himself. "I noticed she doesn't have a ring."

Leif's cheeks colored just a little, and he hurried to finish the measurement he was working on. "I've only been home from my mission for four months. I had to pay for the driving course, and I've been saving up for the ring. We went ahead and got engaged without it." He opened his mouth to say more, perhaps to offer further explanation, but then he stopped himself.

"Don't you think you guys are a little young to get married?" Sam asked, unable to resist playing devil's advocate.

Leif shook his head and smiled. "Delilah's already considered an old maid by Big Fork standards. Most of her friends from high school are married and have a kid or two."

Sam blinked at him. "You're kidding."

Leif shook his head and measured out another length of wood. "We're big on families, and a lot of us get started young. How about you? Are you ever going to settle down?"

"I'm only twenty-three years old," Sam said as he cut another two by four. "I might settle one day, but not for a while."

Leif turned to look at him. "I said settle down, not settle."

He caught that? Sam smiled. "Same thing if you ask me. I mean, I know you and Delilah are hot for each other and have a lot in common, but the romance dies once you shackle yourself to one girl, Leif. It's playing the field that keeps life interesting and keeps the girls trying to impress you. Once they know they've got you, they give up and start looking for the next challenge."

Leif chuckled and shook his head. "You and I are different kind of men, Sam. I consider myself lucky to have found a woman like Delilah. She was the first girl I ever kissed, and she'll be the first and last woman I ever sleep with. We're going to spend our lives raising our children, working, and growing together. I believe that every year will get better, that I'll grow to love her more and more with time. I can't think of anything more romantic than that."

Sam's jaw dropped open. "You mean, you've never . . . been with a woman? Not even Delilah?"

Leif shook his head and gave Sam a strong look. "And I'm proud of that fact." He leaned back and gave Sam his full attention. "We believe that sex is sacred, and I'll guarantee that it will be far more powerful for me than it has ever been for you, because I respect the moment more than you ever could. The commitment we make goes beyond this life, Sam. It's about forever— eternity—and we treat it as such."

I am on another planet, Sam thought to himself. They were all aliens. In fact, he was sure he could hear the space ship circling overhead. "Hmmm," Sam said, turning his focus to the next cut he was supposed to make. "I happen to like playing it my way."

"And we like playing it our way."

Whatever, freak, Sam thought to himself. "Sounds like you and Delilah are meant to be," he said again.

Leif turned back to his tape measure. "Yes, I believe we are."

Sam merely smiled. What simpletons these people were.

They worked for several more minutes, measuring and sawing as needed. Finally they started putting up the frame of the shelves. They anchored the two-by-fours to the walls of the shed by drilling thick screws through the wood. From there they would build the rest of the framework and then put up the shelves. Leif did most of the drilling, although Sam knew he could handle it, if Mr. Control Freak would give him a chance.

"Leif?"

Both men turned to see Delilah standing in the doorway. Before Leif had arrived, she didn't wear any makeup, and her hair was sloppily pulled away from her face. Now she wore her hair in two braids and had a little makeup on. Sam shook his head at yet another example of her neurosis. But Leif had answered some questions about why she wasn't attracted to Sam. She was a virginal nut case. She wouldn't know how to find him attractive if she wanted to. The thought was irritating, and it didn't sit well with him, so he began fantasizing about all the women who threw themselves at him on a regular basis. One little farm girl made no difference in the grand scheme of things.

Leif turned and smiled deeply at his bride-to-be.

She took a few steps into the shed. "You know that pump that was sounding funny this morning?" Leif nodded. "Well, Dad decided to fiddle with it, and he needs some help. Are you at a stopping point?"

"Oh, sure," Leif said. He stood up and laid the drill back in its case.

"I can keep drilling," Sam offered. He'd love to have some time to himself, not to mention the opportunity to show everyone that he could do more than spray cow manure and kill chickens.

Leif looked at Delilah and she shrugged. Sam felt the anger boil. "It's a drill, not a grenade launcher. When I played Max in *Turbo Lover*, I used a drill all the time—I can handle it."

"Okay," Leif said. "Just drill on the little x's. I'll be back as soon as I can."

"Take your time," Sam said with an I-can-do-anything shrug. "I've got this covered." He wasn't sure, but he thought Delilah rolled her eyes. But that was nothing new.

As soon as they were gone, Sam grinned, picked up a screw, and then stared at the drill in consternation. Sure he'd used a drill in *Turbo Lover*, but he'd never actually put the screw in by himself. He looked at the top of the screw and then at the tip-toppy thing on the drill. Their patterns matched. Of course. Holding the drill so that the tip-toppy thing was facing up in the air, he placed the screw on it—a perfect fit. Until he put the drill down. Then the screw clattered to the floor. Wasn't it supposed to stick on there? He tried again and again, then he tried holding the screw on the little x marked on the wood and putting the drill into it. That worked better. It was hard to line the screw up exactly, but he got close enough. Nothing to it.

The first board was done, and he stepped back to admire his handiwork. His screws weren't quite as straight and flush with the wood as Leif's. But they weren't that bad. He rested the drill on his shoulder and pressed the trigger a couple of times in celebration. "I am a God," he said out loud. "I can do anything!"

Then he moved to the next beam, grabbed a screw, and went to lower the drill from where it was still resting on his shoulder. His head burned when he tried the put the tool down. With horror he realized it was stuck in his hair. With his right hand he reached across his shoulders and tried to release what he thought was one section of hair, but his fingers told him a different story. His entire ponytail, or most of it, was tangled around the spinny part of the drill. He didn't know how it happened or why it happened, but surely it wouldn't be hard to undo. He pulled at one strand and then another. The hair held fast, and he felt just a glimmer of panic rise in his chest. He tried squeezing the trigger of the drill again and felt the pull get tighter.

He cursed under his breath and kept trying to free himself from the drill, dreading the reaction he was going to get if he had to ask for help from these people. This was not the way it was supposed to happen!

Mary pulled the big silver mixing bowl out from under the mixer and dumped the mound of dough onto the floured counter top. With a knife she cut it into four sections and then molded each section into a loaf shape. Three of the loaves went into bread pans. The other one was going to become breadsticks for dinner tonight.

After placing a thin cloth over the loaves, she began shaping the breadsticks and laying them on a baking sheet. She looked up when the back door opened and shut.

Sam ran in, his eyes wild-looking as he approached.

"Whatever is the matter?" Mary asked, and then she saw the drill and the hair wadded around it. "Oh my, how did you do that?"

"I don't know," Sam complained. "I was putting up the beams for the shelves in the shed, and I rested the drill on my shoulder. Next thing I knew . . . this had happened."

Mary walked around him, inspecting the predicament. She tried to pull on the hair, but it wouldn't budge.

"Maybe if we reverse the drill," she said. Taking the drill from Sam's hand, but keeping it close to his head so as not to hurt him, she found the button that reversed the direction of the spin. She pulled on the trigger. Sam groaned as it got tighter. She tried it again, and he begged her to stop.

"It's only getting worse," he said, still grimacing with pain. "I've got to get this thing off of me."

"Oh dear," Mary muttered.

"There's got to be something we can do!" Sam said, increasingly concerned with the outcome of this situation. His hair was his signature—his essence. Just then, he heard a loud snip, and the pressure on his hair follicles relaxed. For an entire second he was frozen, then he turned and looked at the hair-laden drill Mary was holding. He reached up and fingered what was left of his hair and felt all the blood drain from his face.

Leif finished his final adjustments on the pump and signaled Rhett to start it up. The consistent whirr that greeted them was music to their ears.

"You're amazing," Rhett said as he clapped Leif on the back. "I swear you can fix anything."

Leif nodded, acknowledging the compliment, and handed the wrench to Delilah, who put it back in the tool box.

Just then a high-pitched scream shattered the stillness and made Delilah's hair stand on end. Even the cows seemed affected by it as they looked up from their feed. The three of them looked at one another and in unison turned and ran toward the house. Delilah's heart was pounding, and she couldn't imagine what would possibly make her mother scream like that.

They were breathless by the time they got into the house. From the back door Delilah could see her mom backed against the wall.

"Mary?" Rhett called as soon as they entered the house. "Mary, are you okay?"

"It wasn't me," she said in a shaky voice. She looked at Sam, and the others followed her lead.

Sam was pale, and his mouth hung open. He looked at Mary as if she were an ax murderer. Delilah looked back at her mother and noticed for the first time the drill wrapped in long brown hair. It only took a second for Delilah to deduce what had happened.

"Oh my gosh," she said.

Sam turned to look at her, his expression blank. "She cut my hair off," he said in a shaky voice. "She whacked it all off."

Delilah looked at her mother. Mary looked nearly as pale and shocked as Sam did. "His hair was tangled in the drill, I couldn't get it out. It was hurting him and . . . I—I didn't . . . think . . ."

Delilah finished the statement in her head. She didn't think . . . "it was that big a deal" or that "a grown man would scream like he'd been shot." But Delilah also knew that Sam's hair was important, and that he took this very seriously.

"Sam," Delilah whispered, still struggling to find the right words for this. "I'm so sorry."

Sam looked at Mary again and closed his eyes. The left side of his hair was cut off nearly an inch from his head, laying in blunt lines against his scalp The rest of his hair tapered down through the back and the right side still had some original length left. It looked horrible. After a few seconds of silence, Sam opened his eyes again and touched his butchered hair once more as if to verify it was true.

"Do you have any idea what you just did?" Sam said in a menacing whisper. His eyes were wild, and Delilah took a protective step toward her mom. "I spend thousands of dollars on just the right hair care products. I have it colored and deep conditioned every month. The color is perfect, the length is perfect—women love running their fingers through it." He stopped and took a deep breath. "My hair was the one thing that set me apart from every other male sex symbol!" His voice raised to a scream. "Do you have any idea what you just did!"

They were all stunned by his outburst. Delilah blinked and tried to think of how to make it better. She drew a blank and settled for attempting to calm him down. "Sam," she said. "It's going to be okay—"

"It's not going to be okay!" he screamed, stomping his foot so hard the cookie jar lids rattled. "It's my hair!! She may as well have cut off my arm. This hair is on every poster across America; it sold me to the American people. They love it, they love the stupid story about my promising not to cut it. They suck it up like a sponge. Now what am I going to do? How am I going to explain this? I promised the producers of *Samson and Delilah* that I wouldn't cut it until after the Oscars—not that I've ever considered cutting it anyway. I am Samson—you can't cut my hair off!" He started looking around the room like a caged dog. "I . . . I . . . I can't believe this happened. I think I'm going to throw up."

"The American people love you because you're a great actor," Delilah reminded him, trying to help. It didn't work. The anger came back, and he turned on her.

"I'm not a great actor, I'm the best! I've managed to live here for eleven days without killing myself—that's got to be a major acting ability! This is all your fault, Delilah. If you would have just said yes in the beginning, none of this would have happened. But, no, you had to make a *point*. You had to bring me to this hell hole and treat me like a migrant worker! I've shoveled poop and milked cows for eleven days and now this! You've destroyed me, Delilah. The only thing I've learned from being here is that if I had to live like this I would find the nearest cliff and jump to my death. Now I know why people want to escape to the movies and watch me blow up mountains. They are trying to escape the horrible drudgery of their lives!"

"I think you're overreacting, and I *know* you're being very offensive," Leif suddenly cut in.

"Overreacting?" Sam spun around to face the other man. "Do you realize that I have satin sheets at home? I come here and sleep on potato sacks. I can't eat eggs or chicken or drink milk ever again because of coming here. The water tastes like dirt. I'll never look at hamburger the same way again. The mattress in that guest room is stuffed with hay, I swear. And the smell! The smell of this place makes me want to vomit all day every day. I'm surrounded by morons who don't know a thing about who I really am, and now this! I've had it!" His face was red now, and he turned toward the door.

"I'm really sorry," Mary whispered.

Sam spun around. "Don't talk to me!" he screamed.

"That's enough," Rhett said sharply, finally finding his tongue. "Go burn off your anger somewhere else and come back when you can talk civilly.

Sam stormed out the back door. He spotted a four wheeler and jumped on, heading for the far end of the pasture and going as fast as he could until the four-wheeler hit a rock and he lost control. He managed to slow it down before it crashed, but was thrown to the ground where he rolled once before flipping onto his back. For a few minutes every bone in his body hurt. *Bring it on*, he thought to himself. *I hope it kills me and puts me out of my misery!* A few minutes passed, and he could feel the wet coldness of the ground seeping through his clothes. *I guess I'm not paralyzed*, he thought dismally. The pain began to subside, and he moved his arms and legs to make sure he'd suffered no real damage. Everything seemed to be fine. *Bummer!* If he had a major injury, he could leave. Then he wondered why he had to be mortally wounded to get out of here.

He was a grown man, and this hadn't been his idea, so why stick around? In that instant he made his decision and immediately began feeling better. He'd put up with this miserable excuse for a life for eleven days. He'd endured menial labor, tap water, insults and injury, and he'd had enough. Delilah wouldn't go to the Oscars, but who really cared? He would leave this place and never look back—except he would still be leaving without his hair. Fresh anger coursed through his veins, and he slammed his hand into the ground, muddy from all the four wheelers that had driven this path the last few days. His hair!! There would be jokes made because Delilah wasn't on his arm for the Oscars, but they would go away some day. The hair, on the other hand, was going to be a constant source of questioning for a very long time. Every time he did an interview he'd be asked what had happened to his hair. Somehow he'd have to come up with a good story to explain it—he didn't think such a thing existed. He slammed his fist into the ground a second time and yelled all the swear words he'd been holding back. When he finished he felt better and began to shiver from the cold. But he didn't have an escape plan formulated yet, so he refused to get up. He wished Cody were here so he could ask his advice. But Cody would likely tell him to stick it out—what was up with Cody's insistence on this anyway?

He wished he'd never met Delilah Glenshaw.

✭ Chapter Nine ✭

The sound of something motorized got Sam's attention, and he lifted his head enough to see a four wheeler coming toward him. The rider's identity was hard to make out. He let his head drop to the ground and began cursing again under his breath, steeling himself for a nasty confrontation. Maybe they would offer to drive him home themselves.

"You okay?"

He opened one eye and peered up to see Delilah staring down at him with concern. The tone of her voice surprised him. He shut both eyes again. "Go away."

"It's freezing out here, Sam. You need to come inside."

"I'd rather freeze to death."

"You're making too big a deal out of this."

"What's it to you?"

Delilah let out a breath and turned off the four-wheeler. She swung around on the seat so she was facing him. "I'm impressed you held out so long, I really am."

Sam opened one eye again. "What?"

"We call it a 'Dairy Diatribe' or a 'Milking Meltdown.' We all have them. You should have seen the fit I threw after my first few days back. When I left we only had sixty cows. The milkings took about an hour. I come back from New York to find forty additional cattle and only two workers. I tried to call this whole thing off, but my dad gave me a lecture about keeping my word and following through with my responsibilities." Delilah stopped and shook her head. "Mom used to schedule her meltdowns when I was in high school. On the thirteenth day of every month she would harangue us with all the reasons she hated this farm. We just had to take whatever she had to say that day. The trade off was that for the rest of the month she kept her feelings about the farm to herself."

"Baloney," Sam said. "Mary would never do that."

Delilah cocked her head to the side. "Did you just say 'baloney'?"

Sam groaned. "Just go away, Delilah. You proved your point. I'm worthless for real work. I'm a figment of the Hollywood people-maker machine, and I have no value other than pretending to be someone else for money. I get it. You broke me. Now go away."

After ten more seconds he opened one eye again. She didn't look like she was preparing to leave.

"I'm sorry about your hair, Sam. I really am. Mom feels terrible."

Sam snorted.

"And I didn't break you. You gave up. You've put up with so much—I've been really impressed. I bet my dad five bucks you wouldn't last three days."

"Oh, that must be why you continue to insult me every chance you get—cause I'm doing so well."

"That's to keep you humble, and maybe to make it less miserable for me. I hate working the farm."

Sam opened both eyes this time. "What?"

She looked at him. "Why do you think I went to be a nanny in New York? I grew up doing this stuff, Sam. I don't mind doing it now and then, but I hate doing it day after day after day. Dad hasn't worked it this much in years."

"Then why have the farm?" He was thoroughly confused.

"Well, it's been my dad's dream all his life—he grew up in Salt Lake but used to go to his grandpa's farm in Idaho every summer. He loves farm work. My mom was born here in Big Fork, but they didn't move out here until Dad had built up his insurance business. He knew that farming wasn't going to support the family—not with this size of a herd anyway. My two older brothers were in high school then, and getting into trouble. The best way to reform a bad boy is to make him work his tail off. They're too damn tired to do anything else."

"We aren't allowed to curse here," Sam said dryly.

Delilah continued as if he hadn't spoken. "Dad used to

work it every day; he loved it. But then he hurt his back a few years ago and just can't do most of the work anymore. He does what he can, but he's been focusing more on the insurance work these days. We all do our part when we have to, but we usually hire out most of the work."

Sam propped himself up on his elbows. "So you really don't do this all the time?"

"No," she said with a shake of her head. "The farm basically pays for itself. Miguel and Eric have worked with us for years, so we knew we could trust them. My younger brother, Daniel, the one on a mission, is the only one that loves farming like my dad. He's planning to buy it from my folks when he gets back."

Sam couldn't believe what he was hearing. "Do you really not have TV and trade your eggs?"

She smiled. "Farm eggs are healthier, so we actually do trade them for other stuff because people want them. Mom's pretty stoked about not having to worry about it anymore, though. Daniel built the coop for a 4H project when he was in Jr. high. He raised the chickens, and Mom had to take it over when he left on his mission. She's actually going to give the surviving chickens to a neighbor. She wishes she'd thought of leaving the coop unlatched a long time ago."

Sam shook his head. "I can't believe you did this to me."

"Hey, I wouldn't go that far," Delilah said. She kicked his arm lightly. "You did this to yourself. When you told me how 'destroyed' you were by my refusal, I about lost my mind. There is so much more to life than playing the paparazzi and living up to the fantasies people have of you. Everyone learns that eventually, even Hollywood icons I suppose. But you were pretty arrogant about your self-importance. It brought out the worst in me. But I've learned a thing or two from this, too."

"Like what?" Sam asked as he sat up completely. His backside was now totally soaked, and he was shivering. But he didn't want to miss a word of this.

"That you are a real person, with likes and dislikes, good parts and bad parts. You have an incredible amount of determination, and you're not quite as shallow as I thought you were."

"Not quite? Is that the best you can do?"

Delilah shrugged, and they sat in silence for several seconds. "We better get going back to the house before you get hypothermia. What are you doing down there anyway?"

Sam stood and looked around for his four-wheeler. Apparently it had rolled enough times that it ended up on its wheels again. He decided not to tell her about his accident. His right hip hurt and his shoulder was sore, but he'd deal with it. "Do we still have to do all the chores and stuff?" he asked as he headed toward his machine.

"Unfortunately, yes," Delilah answered. She straddled her four-wheeler again and drove slowly alongside him. "But we can all let our hair down a little more now that you know the truth." Her eyes moved to his hair, and he lifted his hand to feel what was left of it. "No pun intended," she added.

He couldn't help but cringe at the reminder, and he still hadn't a clue how he was going to explain it. "Can your mom trim it up for me?" Sam asked.

"She's an awful hairdresser," Delilah said. "That's why we trade eggs with Leif for haircuts."

"Leif?"

"Yeah, he cuts all our hair, and does a mean pencil weave if you're interested. His mom owns the beauty salon in town. I grew up milking cows; he grew up setting perms."

Sam shook his head. "Maybe you guys *are* perfect for each other."

Delilah smiled. "No question about it," she said. As soon as he was settled on his four-wheeler, she sped ahead, and they raced to the house.

Within half an hour of returning to the house, Sam had a whole new look. Leif cut it short, but kept it trendy. It had been years since Sam had short hair, so Leif showed him how to style it. The haircutting experience was painful, though. Sam still didn't know what explanation he was going to give when he went back to his real life. But there was no choice but to accept it, and now that the adrenaline had faded, he could honestly say it wasn't the worst thing that had ever happened to him. The worst thing was cleaning up the chickens.

That evening was the nicest one Sam had experienced since arriving at the farm, second only to the one with the Lakers' game. Mary got pizza in town, and after the evening milking they played poker with Disney face cards and M & M's. At ten o'clock when they were heading off to bed, Rhett announced that he'd called the workers back for the morning milkings. Delilah and Sam would have to hide in the house while they were there, and they weren't covering the evening shift. But at least Sam could start sleeping through the night. Delilah walked Leif out to his truck.

Sam went to bed feeling better than he had in a very long time, even before coming to Utah. It was difficult for him to pinpoint exactly what he was feeling, but he knew it had something to do with this family, the simple schedules, and the satisfaction of a job well done. Funny how he'd never noticed those things until today. He'd been so wrapped up in his misery that they hadn't mattered. And it was nice to have a decent conversation with Delilah again. It resurrected the attractions he'd been trying so hard to suppress since Leif had arrived. She really was quite fascinating. As he drifted off to sleep he couldn't stop thinking about her. Her smile seemed imprinted in his mind, and her laugh echoed in his head. All night long he had dreams about Delilah.

For the next two days they interspersed chores with four wheeler races and poker games. It felt as if they were all on the same team for the first time, and he found satisfaction in his work that he'd never expected. They finished fixing the fences, and Rhett showed Sam how to drive the tractor to start plowing part of the field. In the evenings, they all watched movies together, eating Mary's perfect popcorn and homemade cookies. Sam felt he'd learned as much about real life in those last two days as he'd learned in the previous eleven. He'd never been part of a family before, and the more time he spent with the Glenshaws, the more he felt his future changing—a little. He wasn't going to give up what he did for a living, but he knew that he wanted to feel this in his own home one day. If he was going to achieve that kind of goal he needed to make some changes. He could see what it was that Leif saw in Delilah now, and he knew he wanted much of those same characteristics in a woman some day. He refused to let himself think about Delilah as that woman—but it was difficult not to. She was so different, so unique, and he wanted to hold onto that forever. At night his dreams of Delilah persisted, and during the day he found himself watching her more and more. But Leif was always there. Part of him wanted to win the prize, yet another part—one he'd never noticed before—wanted to see the two of them find happiness together. Trying to reconcile those two feelings was nearly impossible, so he tried to ignore them—it didn't work very well.

After they finished the evening milking on day thirteen, Delilah, Leif, and Sam headed back to the house. Rhett had gone in some time ago for a call with a client. They were planning to watch *Fiddler on the Roof,* and Sam was looking forward to it—go figure!

"The fog sure is thick tonight," Sam commented as he looked around and tried to pick out the landmarks he'd come to recognize. There was always fog at night, but it had never been like this. He could barely see ten feet in front of him. What objects he could see were blurred and odd-looking.

"It is," Delilah commented. She and Leif were walking hand in hand next to Sam. With poetic symbolism, Leif separated Sam from Delilah—always separated. She turned to look at Leif. "Are you sure you want to drive home in this? If you stay, you can be here for Sam's farewell breakfast."

"Well, if you insist," he said. Delilah's eyes brightened. She'd been trying to convince Leif to spend the night at the farmhouse all week. Sam didn't understand why, since Leif had made it abundantly clear that the two of them were perfectly chaste and virtuous. But it was exciting to her, none the less.

Sam found the reminder of his impending departure a bit depressing, and then checked himself. Why would he not want to leave this place? He risked a glance at Delilah, knowing full well she was the reason—but he forced himself not to dwell on it.

Delilah continued, "Remember when we used to play 'Fog Tag' on nights like this?"

Leif nodded and laughed. "That was fun," he said. Then he looked at Sam to explain. "In high school we'd bring our friends out here and play. It's kind of like hide and seek. Mary would have hot chocolate and sugar cookies waiting for us inside when we couldn't stand the cold anymore. It was a blast."

Sam smiled as he imagined twenty teenagers playing in the dark. That was a part of life he'd never had—high school. He'd had tutors and correspondence courses, and he felt a pang of jealousy at what he'd missed out on. Suddenly, out of nowhere, Delilah slapped his arm and yelled, "You're it." Within seconds she and Leif had disappeared.

Sam stood there for a few seconds. "Wait a minute," he hollered into the blinding fog. "Aren't there rules or something?"

Delilah's voice rang back to him, and he knew she wasn't far. But as he turned circles he couldn't see her anywhere. "We have to stay between the barn, the house, and the driveway," she answered. "Leif and I can only move five steps at a time and we can't hide behind anything. If you call out 'Fog' we have to answer 'Tag,' then we can take five steps. After that we can't move until you yell 'Fog' again."

"Kind of like Marco Polo," Leif's voice added.

Let the games begin.

Sam called out "Fog" and two voices answered. He thought he'd have no problem finding them but the fog was like soup. His sense of direction was all messed up, and he had no idea where he was. He had to yell "Fog" nearly every thirty seconds just to be sure he knew which way he was supposed to move. After a few minutes he finally caught Leif. Leif closed his eyes and counted to ten while Sam disappeared. Leif didn't catch Delilah, instead he caught Sam again. For the second time in ten minutes Sam was it. He called "Fog" and listened intently, determined to catch Delilah this time. He heard her voice to his left and hurried toward it, only to find nothing.

"Delilah's taking more than five steps," he called out. No

one answered. *Dang*, he thought to himself. He'd hoped his accusation would cause her to defend herself and give away her location. He knew he was close. "Fog," he called out.

"Tag," came the reply. If he didn't know better he'd have thought Delilah was trying to make her voice sound farther away than it was. He moved to his left again.

"Fog," he called again.

"Tag."

She was close. Leif, however, sounded farther away.

He took a few steps backwards and turned around. Delilah was barely discernable in the thick fog. It took a few more steps in her direction to confirm that she was giving him a dirty look. He expected nothing less.

"Crap," she said as her shoulders slumped. "I guess I'm it." She took a breath and yelled "I'm it, Leif. New game."

"Yes!" Leif's voice echoed back. She shook her head before closing her eyes and started counting. But Sam couldn't make himself leave. She had her hair in two braids and a knit cap was pulled down over her ears. With the grey-white fog behind her as a backdrop, she looked incredibly beautiful. Her cheeks and nose were pink from the cold, and she looked almost fairylike, dwarfed by the heavy down coat and thick scarf she wore. When she opened her eyes he was standing less then two feet away. He didn't recall taking any steps.

"Sam," she said quietly, seemingly startled to find him there. "You were supposed to hide." All those feelings he'd been having and trying to ignore came rushing back, and he couldn't help but do this. It was likely the last time he would get to be alone with her and just in case . . . he had to try.

"I couldn't tear my eyes away from you," he admitted, taking another step forward. "You're breathtaking tonight."

Her brow furrowed, and she backed up. "Sam," she said in a warning tone.

"Delilah," he said, reaching out and taking hold of her arm. "I've never met anyone like you. I . . . I know that you and Leif—"

"We're getting married, Sam. You need to let go of me and

go hide before this gets complicated."

Sam grinned a little half smile and pulled her to him. She didn't resist, and he took full advantage of the opportunity. He lowered his face and touched her lips lightly with his own. A wave of warmth traveled the length of his body and alerted senses he had forgotten existed. Maybe she wasn't as committed to Leif as he had thought. He tried to pull her closer, to deepen the kiss, but she pulled roughly away and took a few steps back. He opened his eyes and looked at her in confusion.

"Leif and I are getting married, Sam. I love him, and you had no right to do that." With that she turned and disappeared into the fog.

She really *didn't* want him. The realization was shocking. Until now Sam had told himself she had really good self-control, but that wasn't it. She really *was* in love with Leif, and she really *wasn't* interested in Sam. It was a hard fact to absorb. A few seconds later she called out. "Hey guys, I'm freezing. I've got to go inside."

Leif's protests rang back. "Oh, come on, Dee. Ten more minutes?"

"I'm not feeling well," she answered. Several seconds later Sam heard the back door shut somewhere off to the right. He didn't move for a long time.

Leif emerged from the darkness. "The house is over here," he said with an innocent smile as he pointed to the right.

Sam forced a smile, feeling guilty and small for what he'd just done. "I wasn't sure," he said.

They started walking together. "I know this place like the back of my hand," Leif continued, oblivious to his companion's silence. "I'm going to harass Delilah for giving up. She just hates being it."

Sam just nodded and wished there was a hole he could crawl into. Once inside he excused himself to his room to pack, unwilling to look either Leif or Delilah in the eye. Mary came and knocked a half an hour later. "Are you going to watch the movie?" she asked.

Sam didn't know what to say. If he stayed in his room they

might suspect something. But he wasn't sure he could handle being out there. Still, tonight was his last night here. Did he really want to spend it alone? "I'll be out in a minute," he called back. "Go ahead and get started without me."

It took several minutes before he felt comfortable joining them. Rhett and Mary sat next to one another on the couch. Leif and Delilah were snuggled up on the floor. Sam felt like garbage and wished he had a chance to apologize. It was hard to concentrate on the movie, and he finally excused himself, saying he was tired. He lay on his bed for a long time, thinking over all the things he'd experienced here. The relationship Leif and Delilah shared was unlike anything he'd ever seen. Their genuine friendship intrigued him, as did Rhett and Mary's relationship. They had so little compared to the excess he'd been raised to depend on, yet they were happier than most people he ever met. Throughout his stay he'd avoided discussing religion at all costs, not wanting to give even the hint of interest. And true to her word, Delilah hadn't pushed it. He was grateful that she hadn't tried to force it on him, but it was impossible not to notice their commitment. It made him feel left out somehow, and not just left out from the Glenshaws. It made him contemplate a larger purpose to life. It was obvious through what they said and how they treated each other that they believed in more than what they had right then. Leif had said he and Delilah planned to be together forever. There was passion in his voice when he said it. But a different passion than Sam would have expected.

The thoughts were disconcerting and uncomfortable, and yet soothing at the same time. Now wasn't the time to make sense of them, but one day, when this was over and he could be completely objective, he planned to really think about these things, these concepts that were so important to the Glenshaws and so foreign to himself.

Around eleven o'clock Sam put an end to his ponderings and decided to get himself something to eat. He hadn't been able to fall asleep and hoped a full stomach would help. Leif was sleeping on the hideabed downstairs, and Sam walked quietly so as not to wake him with creaking floorboards. The house had been quiet for nearly an hour so he felt it was safe. After getting himself a glass of water, he grabbed a few cookies from the plate left on the counter and sat down at the table. It surprised him how badly he didn't want to leave tomorrow. But he was unsure whether that was because he would miss this place and these people or if he was anxious about jumping back into his life without his hair. He still hadn't figured out how he was going to explain it. Cody was going to freak.

A soft footfall behind him caused him to turn. Delilah stood in the doorway and smiled awkwardly. Her hair was loose, and she was wrapped in a big pink robe that said "Princess" on the pocket.

"Can I sit down?" she asked.

"It's your house," Sam said evenly. As soon as she sat down, he spoke without looking up.

"I'm sorry about that kiss, Delilah. You were right, and it was wrong of me to do that."

"It's okay," she said.

His head snapped up. What did she mean by that? Was it an invitation?

She seemed to read his thoughts. "It's not okay as in all right for you to do it. It's okay in that I forgive you for it."

"Oh," Sam said softly. Rejected again.

"Sam," she said, "even if I wasn't head over heels in love with Leif, it would never work for you and me."

That wasn't what Sam wanted to hear, and the rejection cut him to the core. He'd had supermodels tell him to take a hike; he'd done it to many women himself. But to have someone as good and pure as Delilah tell him she didn't want him, made him look at himself from a new perspective. "Why not?" he asked quietly, not wanting to hear her answer but knowing that he needed to.

"We're too different," she said in a sympathetic tone. "We have different values, different goals. I could never live in your world, and you could never live in mine. It's the difference about me that's attractive to you, Sam. I'm a mystery to you—something you can't figure out and can't have. That's what causes the excitement. It wouldn't last—even if we wanted it to."

"Do you want it to?" He looked up and met her eye, pleading for her to say she did. She just shook her head. Another rejection. How many of these was he supposed to take in one night?

"How do you know it wouldn't work?" he challenged.

Delilah shrugged. "I just do."

It wasn't the answer Sam was looking for, but he knew what she meant. What's more, he thought she was probably right. Even though he was attracted to Delilah and found her intriguing, he couldn't quite imagine trying to make a life with her long term. They had only gotten along for three days—what were the chances they could do it full time?

"Did you tell Leif?"

"Not yet," she said. "But I will, after you leave tomorrow. We have no secrets."

"Will he hate me?" For some reason the thought of being hated by a Big Fork, Utah truck driver seemed equal to being voted "Worst Dressed" in *People Magazine*. He didn't want to hurt Leif—and it surprised him to feel so concerned with someone else's happiness.

"I've yet to meet a man that equals the kind of person Leif is. It will bother him, but I'm sure he'll understand and move on."

"Will he still let you go to the Oscars?"

"Of course he will," she said, slapping him lightly on the arm. "That's why we have no secrets, because we trust one another. He's also my very best friend. He wouldn't stop me from going."

Sam cocked his head to the side. "You sound almost excited to go."

Delilah smiled. "I'm getting more excited every day . . . and nervous. My mom picked up some beautiful fabric to make me a new dress—an updated one. And Leif's going to experiment with the perfect hairdo."

"Are you sure I can't talk you into wearing the Versace?"

"No way," she said strongly as she stole one of his cookies. "I do the dress—that's the deal."

"Okay, okay." He met her eyes and smiled. Silence descended for several moments. When Sam spoke again, his voice was soft. "I hope I find a woman like you someday, Delilah."

"Become the kind of man that a woman like me could spend her life with, and you will."

"I've learned a lot being here," he continued. "Thanks for the opportunity."

A huge smile spread across her face. "Now that's something I never thought I'd hear."

✻ Chapter Ten ✻

Sam finished his cookie and went back to his room. Delilah put the dishes in the sink and turned around to find Leif standing in the doorway. She jumped and put a hand to her chest. "You scared me," she said with a little laugh at her own reaction.

Leif wasn't smiling.

"What's wrong?"

"When did he kiss you?" he asked in an even tone.

Delilah took a breath and walked toward him, wanting him to see and hear and feel the sincerity of her answer. She took both his hands in her own and looked him in the eye. "When we were playing 'fog tag.' It was my turn to be it and when I opened my eyes he was standing there. He kissed me—for half a second, before I pulled away and told him to never do anything like that again."

"He could give you a life you'll never have with me," Leif said.

"That's the silliest thing you've ever said to me," she responded. "Don't offend me by thinking I've even entertained the thought. Did you hear everything we said?"

Leif nodded. There was still a question in his eyes. She went up on her tip-toes, pulled him close, and kissed him deeply. When she pulled back, she rested her forehead against his. "I waited for you for two and a half years. I turned down a dozen guys that asked me out. You're my very best friend, Leif. You're the man I'm going to spend forever with. You're the man that's going to take me to the temple and baptize our children. Do you really think I would trade that for anything? The last thing you need to worry about is that I would fall for a man the likes of Sam Hendricks."

Leif took a moment to consider that. Apparently he was satisfied, enough that he changed the subject. "I heard someone up here and hoped it was you. I thought I'd catch some time with you alone."

"You're a naughty boy," Delilah teased before kissing him again.

Leif smiled after she pulled away. "I've been wanting to give you this." He pulled his hand away from hers and twisted a ring from his little finger.

Delilah caught her breath and met his eyes again. "You got the ring?" she said. "I thought it would be awhile longer."

"Well," he said. "When all this broke loose I realized two things. The first was that if there was ever a chance I might lose you, it was now."

"Leif . . . "

He put his fingers on her lips to keep her from talking. "And," he continued, "that you didn't have three months left in your nanny contract."

She looked at him with confusion, then understanding dawned. A smile spread across her face.

"After hearing what you just said, I don't think I need to worry about losing you now." She shook her head before he continued. "And I think we ought to move the wedding date up a little. Why wait until May?"

Delilah laughed, and he put the small ring on her finger. She didn't even take the time to inspect it before wrapping her arms around his neck. "I'm ready when you are," she said.

"Delilah," Leif continued softly, "you're the best thing that ever happened to me."

"I can't imagine spending my life with anyone but you."

He lowered his face, and she held him as tightly as she could.

Cody finished packing the last of his things and loaded them into the Jaguar XL that Barry had sent down from Palm Springs the night before. As he walked through the Malibu beach house on his way to the front door, he looked around one last time. There were aspects of working for Sam that he would miss, like the continual adventures and the energy Sam possessed. But it was hard to imagine he'd miss it too much.

Earlier that day he'd finished the tape he was planning to leak to the press, ending it with the freak-out session over Mary cutting off Sam's hair. They'd captured every moment on tape—Cody had laughed for hours. Now the final cut was finished, and several copies would soon be mailed—anonymously of course—to all the tabloids and magazine shows. By Monday the airwaves would be full of Sam's downfall—at least for awhile. Cody knew the business well enough to realize it wouldn't last forever. If Sam found the right person to spin it for him, he'd likely claw his way back to the top. But Cody was the best, and Sam didn't have Cody anymore.

The smallest flicker of guilt made him second guess his decision. But the choice had been made. Sam had waited too long to give Cody the credit he deserved. Now he would pay dearly. After scouring the house one last time, Cody locked the door and climbed into his new car. He'd already arranged for Ryan, one of Sam's bodyguards, to pick up Sam tomorrow. What happened after that was going to be ugly. Sam would know Cody was involved, but Barry had promised to back him up, so he wasn't worried. All the tapes were locked in a safe-deposit box in Barry's name. Cody would go out in a blaze of glory. Sam was up the proverbial creek with no paddle at all.

The smell of bacon greeted Sam when he awoke the next morning. He rolled over carefully, so as not to fall off the twin sized bed—it had happened more often than he liked to admit. Staring at the ceiling, he tried to get himself excited about going back to Malibu. He thought about sitting on the beach, drinking a beer as the sun went down, and watching an interview of himself on TV. It was a formula for total satisfaction three weeks ago. Right now it was hard to even look forward to it. After several minutes he climbed out of bed and got dressed.

When he entered the kitchen, Mary was putting bacon on a plate. Rhett was mixing orange juice, and Delilah and Leif were setting the table.

"Wow," Sam said with appreciation as he took in the spread of food. OJ, bacon, biscuits, homemade hash browns, and scrambled eggs—which he still couldn't eat. "This is quite a meal."

Mary smiled proudly. "We wanted to send you off with a good breakfast. A man by the name of Ryan called a little bit ago and said he would be picking you up around ten."

Sam looked at the clock. It was not quite nine. Good. He wanted to enjoy this final meal. "I'm glad I didn't sleep in then," Sam said as he sat down. "Did he say why Cody wasn't picking me up?"

Mary shook her head. Within a few minutes everyone was seated. Rhett offered the prayer over the food, adding a few words of good wishes for Sam as he traveled. Then they ate. It was fun and loud, and by the time they finished, Sam didn't want to go at all. He and Leif did the dishes. When they were about half way through, there was a knock at the door. Hands slowed. They all stopped talking and shared looks of disappointment.

"He's early," Sam said as he put one last dish in the dishwasher. He looked around at these four people with whom he had nothing in common and felt emotion rise in his throat. There were hugs all around, even from Delilah, and then everyone said their final goodbyes. It was Sam's acting ability alone that kept him from making a fool of himself. When he finally got into the back seat of the car, he felt very small and very disconnected from everything. The sign promising death to media people passed outside his window, and he faced the full reality that he would never come back here. It was over and done. Delilah would come to the Oscars, but it wouldn't be like this. Part of him said "Thank goodness!" He never wanted to milk another cow or smell another chicken coop for as long as he lived. But another part of him felt incomplete, as if by not coming back he'd miss out on a lot of what life was all about in the first place.

Rhett, Mary, Leif, and Delilah watched the car disappear.

"Well, that's it," Delilah said as the last of the dust settled. She looked at her parents. "Do you think we did him any good?"

Rhett smiled. "Anything we share with someone else, when it's given in love, blesses their life. I think he will be a better man because of this."

They nodded and turned back to the house. Just as they reached the back door, Mary stopped in her tracks. Rhett, Delilah, and Leif looked at her in surprise.

"What's the matter, dear?" Rhett asked.

"I forgot to remind him to send me that autographed *Rolling Stones* cover."

Delilah groaned and continued into the house. "Mom," she said with a shake of her head.

Rhett and Leif shook their heads, too.

"Do you think he'll forget?" she continued as she followed them. "You've got his number—can we call him?"

⭐⭐⭐

Trisha P was awake with the sun and immediately got ready for her Saturday morning walk. Her husband, Jared Pompiskoloski, was a late sleeper, whereas she preferred to jump into the day before anyone had the chance to mess it up.

After pulling on her walking shoes, she grabbed a light sweater and jogged out the front door. She only kept up the pace for half a block or so; then she walked the remainder of the two-mile walking path that circumvented the gated Palm Springs community where she kept her weekend house.

It wasn't practical to live here all the time, not if she wanted to continue running her production company and news program. But every Friday afternoon she and Jared escaped the tumult of downtown LA and enjoyed the nicest place on earth, or at least in California—Palm Springs.

The community in which their house was located was

complete with its own pool, golf course, and restaurant. Her neighbors were all Hollywood minions—producers, directors, and an occasional corporate CEO. There were a few TV personalities like herself, but they were the minority. Most of the population consisted of behind-the-scenes personnel that made enough money to enjoy this kind of lifestyle. She loved that no one acted shocked or awestruck when they saw her, and the gates and guards kept it safe to go outside.

She finished the first mile and stepped up the pace to a brisk walk, hoping to get home in time to fix Jared breakfast. As she walked, a hundred "to do's" cycled through her mind. She sighed with frustration. It was impossible to get away from her job, no matter how hard she tried. After twenty years she ought to be used to it. This Thursday would be her annual Oscar preview. She would review the films boasting multiple nominations, interview some of the actors and producers, and report on the big Oscar stories. In years past the big stories had been *The Blaire Witch Project*, *My Big Fat Greek Wedding*, and *Lord of the Rings*. She'd also covered the scandals or other issues surrounding the event.

This year the big gossip story was Sam and Delilah. She had a great segment put together, highlighting Delilah's public refusal and then her press conference acceptance. In fact, she'd been trying to get in touch with Sam, in hopes that she could get a little more information, but he hadn't been returning her calls—not even his assistant, Cody Jenkes, had called her back. It hadn't escaped her notice that all Sam's recent interviews had been taped, but after all the hoopla he'd likely taken a break. Still, it bothered her. Everyone returned *Trisha's* calls, even if they were on vacation. Trisha had even tried to get an interview with Delilah, but she was locked up tight in some island resort and no one—not even Trisha P—could get to her there.

Oh well, she thought to herself with a mental shrug. The piece was excellent as it was. And maybe Sam would return her call this week. She could work in an interview, so long as he called by Wednesday.

Her thoughts moved to other topics, other shows she needed to put together, and other calls she needed to make. She rounded a turn in the path and noticed a man ahead of her. Moving to the right of him, so as to pass when she caught up, she increased her pace even more. He was walking much slower than she was and seemed to be looking around, soaking up his surroundings. Maybe he was new.

As she pulled along side of him, she turned to smile and wish him a good morning. When he saw her, his eyebrows went up, as did hers. He immediately looked away.

"Mr. Jenkes?" she asked as she slowed her pace. Her thoughts immediately returned to her earlier ponderings on Sam Hendricks.

He looked back and gave her a brief smile, but he avoided her eyes and her newswoman antenna went up. "Good morning, Trisha," he said with what sounded like forced casualty.

"What are you doing here?" she asked, now keeping step with him. "Sam didn't buy a house here, did he?" There weren't many stars as big as Sam that preferred the community feel of this complex, so she considered it unlikely. Maybe they were just staying with a friend—but she would have known. He couldn't hide in Palm Springs, especially not in her own neighborhood. So then, why was Cody here? Sam was well-known for keeping his assistants on a short leash.

Cody's reply took too long, and her antenna started scanning. "No, Sam didn't buy a house here."

"Oh," she said slowly. "So who are you here with?" It was a direct question that required a direct answer. Few people could pull off such questions—but she could. She did it for a living.

"Um, I just moved in, actually."

Her eyebrows raised again. "You did?"

Cody nodded, and she could tell that he was trying not to appear as uncomfortable as he really was. "And I'm not working for Sam anymore. I'm working with Barry Bradshaw."

"Really," Trisha said in long, even tones. The way she said it demanded that he answer with a little more detail.

"You know how Sam is—he can't keep an assistant for long."

"No, he can't," Trisha commented. She continued to pin him down with her eyes.

"I was ready for a change."

Trisha nodded. There was a story here; she could taste it. But then her good angel rose up on her shoulder and warned her of being paranoid. Actors changed assistants almost as often as they changed girlfriends. It wasn't that unusual. But it didn't change the fact that Sam Hendricks hadn't made a public appearance in nearly two weeks. His interviews had all been taped, and he wasn't returning her calls. Now his assistant had quit. Something was going on.

But she couldn't give herself away too much. She smiled. "Well, I hope it works out with Barry. He could use someone like you."

"I hope so, too," Cody said with a smile. He relaxed now that the encounter seemed to be over. They stood in silence for a few seconds. "Well, I was only walking a short ways, to get a feel for the place. I think I'll head back." He turned and started walking in the direction he had come.

"I hope you like it here," Trisha called after him. He turned and waved before walking off.

Trisha started walking again, trying to convince herself to stop thinking about the encounter. It was the weekend, her time off. There were better ways to spend her time than to wonder about the comings and goings of personal assistants. But there were too many unanswered questions. She promised herself, right then and there, that she would let it sit until the weekend was over. She would not obsess! But come Monday morning . . .

Ryan dropped Sam off around midnight. The house was dark and empty. When Sam had asked about Cody, Ryan said he didn't know why Cody had called him to do the pick up. Cody had simply said he was unable to make the trip. Once inside, Sam dropped his bags on the marble floor of the entryway.

Cody stayed in one of the guest rooms at the back of the house. Sam knocked lightly on the door. After getting no reply, Sam decided not to wake him. He couldn't count the times he'd demanded that Cody get up in the middle of the night for one reason or another, but he felt badly about doing it now. There was nothing he had to say that couldn't wait until tomorrow.

His footsteps sounded loud as he walked up the thick marble stairs that led to his room. At the top of the stairs he turned and looked down on his polished beach house. A Rishard May painting was hung over the leather couch. A Baccarat vase was filled with silk lilies. Everything was beautiful and perfect and . . . depressingly cold. He tried to imagine playing M & M poker in the kitchen . . . but who would he play it with? Cody would play with him, he supposed, but only because Sam paid him, not because Cody would want to. Curling up on the marble floor to watch *Fiddler on the Roof* was out of the question. If the Glenshaws were to come here, they would find it to be nothing like the home they were used to. He hated that realization.

The morning sun greeted Sam full in the face at six A.M.. He muttered cursings on Cody for not having lowered all the black-out blinds yesterday in anticipation of this very thing. It seemed as if Cody had gotten lazy in Sam's absence. After showering and getting dressed, he went downstairs to see what the chef had left for his breakfast. His chef, Enrico, only worked Tuesday thru Saturday. For Sunday and Monday Sam had to make do with whatever leftovers Enrico had saved for him. As he entered the kitchen area, he tried to ignore how empty it felt. It was weird to feel so awkward in his own house, and he didn't like it. The bright sun was a blinding contrast to the gray winter mornings in Utah—and he missed the fog and gloom in a very odd and disconcerting way.

In the fridge, he found some mini quiches—perfect. He heated them in the microwave and refused to dwell on the fact that they were made from eggs. Surely the chef had used white eggs. White eggs seemed so much cleaner. Apparently Cody was sleeping in, or he hadn't realized that by not lowering

Sam's shades, Sam would be up earlier than usual. There was no coffee in the pot, but Sam was in a generous mood. He decided to let Cody sleep and make it himself. The second pot turned out just fine.

Once his little breakfast was hot, he took it to the table. It was a lone ly meal, and he was sorely tempted to wake Cody up just to have some company. Funny how eating by himself hadn't b o t h e red him before. To create the illusion that he wasn't alone, Sam picked up the remote and turned on the TV, which was set to the weather station. He watched it for a few minutes, noting that it looked like the Glenshaws were still immersed in fog. The coffee tasted particularly bitter, and he added some sugar . . . and some creamer . . . and some more sugar, until it tasted a lot more like hot cocoa than coffee. He made a mental note to have the chef buy some hot chocolate the next time he went to the store. Or maybe he'd send Cody out for some when he got up. *Why isn't he up anyway?* Sam wondered. Surely, he'd heard Sam moving around. These bad habits he'd fallen into were going to demand some attention.

The weather moved to the east coast, which he had no interest in, so he flipped the channel and took another sip of coffee. When he looked up from his mug, he started, and the coffee went down his wind pipe. There on the TV was a grainy image of a half-sheared maniac screaming at the top of his lungs while a scared woman hugged a hair-covered drill to her chest. Sam couldn't stop coughing and he couldn't hear what was being said, but it was familiar enough that he didn't need to.

Once he finally stopped choking, he turned up the sound. There was footage! Someone had taped his experience in Big Fork. It was on national TV! His head started to spin as full realization dawned. The whole horrible hair experience was there, down to his scathing explanation of his hair meaning nothing to him—he only kept it to impress his fans. He could hardly breathe. *Cody!* he thought as he spun out on the tile, trying to run to the other man's room. Cody would know what to do about this.

Throwing the door open, he was halfway through his plea

for help when he realized that Cody wasn't there. The closet door hung open. The bed was stripped down to the mattress. There was no cologne on the dresser, no personal items anywhere in fact. Sam did a very slow scan of the room and finally saw a single piece of paper taped to the TV. Sam walked to the television and pulled it off the screen. His heart slowly descended to his toes.

This explains it all—press 'play.'

Sam turned on the TV, then looked around and found the play button on the VCR. In grainy color, just like the show in the other room, he watched Delilah and Leif sitting at the table. They were discussing Delilah's press conference. He couldn't remember the exact context of this scene. Then he watched his long-haired self walk into the room and sit down. That's when he remembered.

"Here, Cody," he said on the tape a few minutes into the playback. "Here, Cody-Cody-Cody."

Sam slowly sank to the bed and watched the conversation talk its way out. He rewound it and played it again.

Several things became apparent as he finished up the second viewing of the tape. The first was that he was in serious trouble. He had no assistant and . . . no date. His stomach burned as he imagined how Delilah and her family were going to react. His promise that no one would ever know he'd been there had been broken. He tried to think of solutions, but he drew a blank. He stood to leave the room, sick to his stomach and sick at heart. On the nightstand next to the bed he saw his cell phone. He picked it up and turned it on. There were one hundred and fifty nine messages.

That's odd, he thought to himself. There were very few people that had this number. It only took listening to the first five messages to realize that Cody hadn't stopped at leaking the tape. His phone was full of messages from different press people asking for his comments. Sam stopped listening to the messages and dialed his attorney.

✮ Chapter Eleven ✮

Delilah paced back and forth as she mentally ranted and raved. It was now Wednesday, four days since the tapes of Sam's stay had hit the airwaves. She was ready to lose her mind. The most intense of the media had left, but a few die-hards were still hanging around town, talking to her old elementary school teachers and the clerks at the grocery store about what her favorite foods were. Not having TV, Delilah didn't know much about what was being shown the world, but she knew very well what had been caught on tape. Rhett and Mary had seen the first of the reporters parked at the front gate when they came home from church on Sunday. As soon as they got into the house they looked it up on the Internet. It wasn't hard to put the pieces together as they scoured the kitchen for the camera. It was hidden in the eye socket of Mary's Snoopy cookie jar. The three of them had stared at the evidence, and then the rage had begun to boil. Within an hour the house had become their prison. Leif's parents' house was also under siege. Even though he was only a few miles away, he and Delilah could only communicate by e-mail, thanks to the press camped outside their houses. They didn't dare leave their property and the phones had been off the hook since Sunday. For four days the only thing any of them had been able to do was rally themselves against Sam Hendricks.

Then an idea came to Delilah. "What if I held another press conference?" she said out loud. Mary and Rhett were outside doing chores to work off their frustration, so she was only talking to herself. But she continued despite her lack of audience. "From what I've found on the Internet, Sam hasn't said anything about it. And they still think I'm his date for the Oscars. Maybe I need to get up there and tell the truth before Sam figures out how to make this work for his benefit." She waited a few minutes and pondered the option. Then she went outside and rallied the troops.

It took half an hour for Rhett, Mary, Leif, and herself to gather the remaining press and journalists. Nearly half a dozen had cameras, and the conference would be spread across the nation by the end of the day. She held the impromptu conference in the Big Fork city offices.

It took ten minutes to explain the real story. She started at the beginning, in Central Park. She explained how she'd been fired, how she and Sam had made an agreement—one he had since broken. In meticulous detail she explained her reasons for the trade. "I am not a celebrity watcher. I don't read *People Magazine*, and I've never even watched the Oscars on TV. Pop culture has nothing to do with my reality, and I wanted to show him that.

"I felt it was a fair trade—until now. It has become apparent that Sam Hendricks is even less of a man than I thought he was. It's obvious that what happened here was simply one more opportunity to manipulate America and humiliate me. I never wanted any of this. I respectfully ask that the media leave me and my family alone. Please try to understand that we are just normal people trying to live our lives the best way we know how."

Trisha P watched the press conference from her office at T studios in LA. She had followed the story very closely, trying to piece it together. She had tried calling Sam again, but he wasn't returning her calls. He had filed a lawsuit against Cody on Monday afternoon, alleging that Cody had planted the camera without his knowledge. She wasn't certain that Sam hadn't paid him in advance to do it and then arranged for Cody to quit so that they could make it appear as if Sam had nothing to do with it. But there were a few holes in that theory.

For one thing, Sam was making absolutely no statements to the press other than that he had no knowledge of the camera.

Sam always sucked the press for all it was worth. His silence was intriguing. But the aspect that caught her attention the most, lending Sam credibility in the process, was that the clips showed him in such a negative light. If Sam had had any part in it, he'd have made sure that the images "leaked" to the press showed him well. They didn't. He looked like a total fool, and his offensive statements infuriated people. Sam would never agree to something like that.

With those things in mind, she was brought back to her encounter with Cody on Saturday. He'd been so uncomfortable, so hesitant to look her in the eye. It seemed to her that if he and Sam had been in on this together, he'd have little reason to act that way in her presence. In fact, it would have made more sense for him to give her some hint of what was coming, perhaps try to solicit an interview. Then again maybe he was as good an actor as his former employer.

That led to another hole. Cody was already working for Barry Bradshaw. Would he jump into new employment so fast if Sam was giving him some kind of payoff?

Then, of course, there was Delilah Glenshaw. Would Sam spend two weeks on a dairy farm, just to leak the tapes one week before the Oscars, knowing full well that Delilah wouldn't go with him? Why not wait until after the Oscars, milking the Delilah story to its hilt, then leak the tapes? It just didn't add up.

When the press conference ended she called Sam again, and again it went to his voice mail. She left another message. After hanging up the phone she tapped it against her chin as she tried to come up with a plan.

"Doris," she called over her shoulder. Her secretary stuck her head in the doorway.

"Yes?"

"Find me the number for Barry Bradshaw—I need to talk to his new assistant."

The evening after the press conference, just hours after the press had scurried back to the holes they had climbed out of with the story clutched in their sticky little fingers, Leif and Delilah were finishing up wedding plans at the Glenshaws' kitchen table. Leif was leaving in the morning on his last long haul and they were trying to make the best of their final moments. They finished everything they needed to discuss, and Leif turned to look at Delilah with a thoughtful expression. "There's one thing that doesn't quite make sense."

"What's that?" Delilah asked as she closed the three-ring binder that served as their wedding planner.

"We all agree that Sam is arrogant and self-serving, right?"

Delilah turned to look at him. She didn't want to discuss Sam and wished Leif hadn't brought it up. "Is there any doubt?"

"So, if he was behind the filming, why would they use clips that show him in the worst possible way? Granted, there weren't a lot of favorable clips—but there were plenty that made him look better than those they're showing."

"So, what exactly are you saying?" Delilah asked, pushing the binder away. She rested her elbows on the table and rested her chin on her hands. "You think he was telling the truth about not having anything to do with it?"

Leif shrugged. "It's possible."

Delilah didn't want to consider that, but the idea wasn't easy to ignore. "Or he just left it up to someone stupid. At the press conference someone said that Cody quit. I think Sam fired him for choosing such lousy clips to leak."

"But can you think of any worse clips that could have shown up? Those segments had to have been the most awful moments."

"So his plan backfired." She shrugged and leaned back in her chair.

"Or he didn't know about it."

"I hate even thinking that."

"Why?" Leif asked.

"Because meeting him screwed up my life, and I want to hate him for it."

"Did it screw up your life?"

Delilah sighed in exasperation. "Why are you defending him?"

"I'm not defending him," Leif said with a shake of his head. "I just want to be fair."

"Fair?" Delilah snorted. "What's fair about any of this? I'm supposed to be in New York saving money for us to put a down payment on a house we're not going to get now. Instead I'm . . . " her voice trailed off.

"Here, with me?"

"That's enough," Delilah said with sincerity, although there was no anger in her voice. "I won't tolerate your defending him and saying this all worked out for the best."

"So you're saying it didn't work out for the best?"

Delilah hated this side of her fiancé. Leif had a way of pointing out the things she didn't want to see. "Leif," she said with exasperation. "The fact is that Sam and I made a deal, and it was broken. I shouldn't give in. The man doesn't need anything to inflate his ego."

"I agree with that," Leif said. "But if you ignore what this does to his ego, and if you give him the benefit of the doubt and assume he didn't have anything to do with the camera or the tapes—if you ignore all that, doesn't part of you want to go?"

Delilah looked at him in shock. "You think I should go?" she said. "You think after all that's happened, I should go to the Oscars with Sam Hendricks?"

Leif shrugged. "How many people get a chance to step into another world like that?"

"I can't believe you're even saying this," she said with a shake of her head. "I would think that you, of all people, would not want me to spend an evening hanging on Sam's arm."

"Sam doesn't threaten me," Leif said with a laugh that seemed to say the very thought was preposterous. "And it would be a great story to tell our kids someday."

Delilah shook her head. "You never cease to amaze me," she said.

Leif stood and pulled her to her feet. "Good. Once you

figure me out, I'll be boring. So what do you think?"

"I think . . . that I need to think about this a little longer."

"Fair enough," he said, and kissed her before announcing he needed to leave.

"I hate that you're leaving again," she said.

"Me, too."

"When will you be back?"

"Four weeks."

"And then no more long haul?"

"None."

Delilah sighed and rested her head against his shoulder. "I'm going to miss you."

"Enough that you can have the wedding ready when I get back?"

She smiled and tried to absorb the smell of him—the feel of being in his arms. Having him so close these past weeks made it even harder to let him go. It had been two and half years since they'd had so much time together. Her stomach hurt in anticipation of his leaving again.

She pulled back. "So you're leaving me to make the decision about Sam on my own?"

"Of course not," he said jokingly. "I'm behind you all the way."

Long after Leif was back on the road and the house was quiet, Delilah slipped into the kitchen. She was in search of the leftovers of the peach cobbler she'd made for dessert that night. After heating it in the microwave, she added a scoop of ice cream and sat down at the kitchen table.

Thanks to Leif she couldn't sleep. She put a spoonful of cobbler in her mouth and realized she was sitting in the same seat she'd sat in when Sam apologized for the kiss. Her thoughts wandered back to the conversation, and it made her wonder why it *had* only been the lousy moments that showed up on TV. Her eyes drifted to the phone, and she considered calling Sam right then and asking him herself. But she hated backing down! Regardless of Leif's suspicions, Sam had broken their agreement. He deserved to live with the consequences.

She finished the cobbler and went back to her bedroom. Mary hadn't done the final touches on the dress, but it was finished exc ept for the zipper up the back and the hem around the bottom. It took less than a minute for Delilah to slip out of her sweats and into the dress. Holding the back together with one hand, she twisted in front of the mirror and appraised her mother's handiwork. The dress was red satin, with a damask pattern on the bodice and sweetheart neckline. It had a corset-type support in the top and a long flowing skirt that swept the ground when Delilah walked. Mary had spent nearly every minute of free time on it. It was a beautiful dress and it accented Delilah's figure perfectly. She felt bad that it would never be worn. Red had always been a great color on her, and she stared at herself in the full-length mirror far longer than she should have.

"Am I really considering this?" she asked herself out loud a few minutes later. No answer came immediately, but she knew that meant that anything was possible. However, she wasn't ready to commit either way . . . yet. The very idea that she was considering going made her take off the dress and hide it in the closet again. She was insane!

Sam had stayed inside his estate for five days. He had thrown his cell phone against the wall after that first conversation with his attorney. It didn't work when it was in four pieces. Weird. The phone number to the house had been changed, but he hadn't given it to anyone. What was the point? He wasn't sure he could trust anyone enough to warrant talking to them. He'd called Enrico and told him to take a week off. Sam had become pretty good at fixing himself peanut butter and jelly sandwiches, so he could fend for himself. For once in his life he didn't want company. The days had been filled with a lot of introspection and thoughts about his future that he had seldom taken time to consider—other than what awards he'd like to decorate his mantle with. He hadn't hired a new assistant either. It was the first time in nearly ten years that he'd had this much time to himself.

Thursday morning he went for a walk on his beach, careful not to go too close to the end of his property, in case the paparazzi was hiding there. Then he went inside and fixed himself some coffee, loaded with cream and sugar. The buzzer from his front gate sounded, and he rolled his eyes. Surely the press knew better than to request entrance. He got up from the table and went to the intercom.

"I am not accepting visitors, and I can sue you for hitting that button!"

He let go of the button and turned away. "Sam, it's Trisha P—I need to speak to you."

Sam paused, surprised that she would be here. Turning back to the intercom he pushed the button again. "Trisha P, how do I know it's you?"

There were a few seconds of silence before she spoke again. "Stop fidgeting—you'll make the director nervous."

It *was* Trisha P! "Make sure no one follows you in," Sam said as he pushed the button that opened the big iron gates. Less than a minute later there was a knock at his door. He opened it and stared at her for a moment before letting her in.

"This is a beautiful home," she said as she looked around the perfectly coordinated and decorated rooms. Sam folded his arms across his chest and tucked his hands under his armpits as he looked around himself.

"It's rather cold and uninviting if you ask me," he said. "I'm considering having it redone, bring in some woods and soothing fabrics."

Trisha turned and looked at him with a surprised smile on her face. "More like that little house in Utah?"

Sam's expression hardened. "I'm not going to discuss it," he said. "Not with you, not with anyone."

"Why ever not?" Trisha asked. "This isn't like you, Sam."

Sam shrugged and said nothing.

"I can give you an exclusive interview. I'll include it in the Oscar Preview show tomorrow night, and you'll get a chance to explain yourself to the world the night before the Oscars. The very fact that you appear on my show will lend you credibility—you know that."

"I'm not going to discuss it," Sam said again. "I gave my word."

"Oh pish," Trisha said with a dismissive gesture. "I know the Glenshaws have already filed suit against you. Delilah did a press conference, and you've said nothing. It just makes you look guilty."

Sam regarded her for a few seconds and cocked his head to the side. "It makes me *look* guilty? Don't you think I *am* guilty?"

"Do you mean to ask if I really think you would leak tapes of yourself looking like a buffoon—no, I don't think you'd do that. Whether you had any part in the filming is still a matter of debate."

Sam shook his head and let out a breath. "Cody wanted to plant a camera. I said absolutely not. As far as I was concerned it was over. As far as he was concerned it had just begun."

"I saw Cody, you know. In Palm Springs. Barry Bradshaw gave him a house."

Sam nodded. "Good, I hope it works out for him." He'd come to accept that he'd treated Cody with far less respect than he deserved. Not that it made what he'd done okay, but Sam could see, for the first time ever, just how much power assistants had and why it was important to treat them accordingly. In fact, he was surprised none of them had turned on him before now.

"I also talked to him on the phone last night," Trisha continued.

Sam raised his eyebrows. "You did?"

Trisha nodded. "I negotiated something for you—if you're interested."

"What?" Sam said, unable to keep the suspicion out of his voice.

"Cody agreed to give you the originals of the tapes in exchange for you not proceeding with the lawsuit."

Sam blinked and thought it through. His initial thought

was that by not following through with the lawsuit he'd simply encourage the belief that he was behind this. But to get the tapes back—to spare himself and the Glenshaws continued embarrassment—that was a powerful temptation. In that instant he had the choice between revenge and protection. It was an easy choice. "I'll do it if he'll give me all his copies, sign a contract to that end, and never speak about the terms of my stay in Utah. I want this to go away," he said strongly. "When can you get them?"

"This afternoon."

Sam hesitated. "What's in it for you?"

"Helping a friend," Trisha said as she turned toward the door. "I'll let you know if I think of anything you can do to make it up to me."

"I won't give you an interview, Trisha," he said with finality. "I won't discuss it, so if you're offering this to me in hopes of an interview, then we may as well stop right here."

"Okay, I understand," she replied.

"One more thing," Sam said as she put her hand on the doorknob. "Will you send them to Delilah?"

Trisha's brow furrowed. "What?"

"Not now, not until after the Oscars," he said. "But next week, will you send them to her? I want her to know that she doesn't have to worry about them anymore. And tell her I didn't know about the camera. She won't believe you, but I'd feel better if you'd tell her anyway."

Trisha nodded. "Who are you taking to the Oscars in her place?"

"I'm not going."

"Really?"

"I'm making a point," Sam explained. "Delilah was my date—and no one can replace her. She's an amazing girl, Trisha. It's a shame you never got to meet her."

Trisha turned to face him one more time. "I could take her the tapes today and tell her you didn't know. She could be here tomorrow."

Sam shook his head. "Then it would seem like I was bribing

her. The deal was broken; her family has been through enough. She owes me nothing. This isn't about me. It's about her, about making it right."

"And they say Hollywood has no values anymore."

"When I look at it from Delilah's perspective, I wonder about that myself."

Before Trisha left, Sam gave her his new phone number so that she could tell him when the tapes were sent. He asked that she give the number to Delilah and hoped that Delilah would call him afterwards, just so they could talk about things. Trisha promised she would before the door shut behind her. Sam felt lifted by the visit and was glad he'd let her in. He could only hope that the tapes would help plead his case. There was really nothing more that he could do.

When Trisha got back into her car, she told the driver to go, and removed the small silver pin she had fastened to her lapel. Then she dialed a number on her cell phone as she closed her fist around the disguised microphone.

"Did you get all that?" she said into the phone.

"Every word."

"Good."

There was a knock at the Glenshaws' door Saturday afternoon, and Delilah looked up with alarm. The door had become her enemy. She was in the middle of kneading bread—anything to help work out the frustrations she felt with having Leif gone and the continual question of what, if anything, she should do about Sam and the Oscars—only a day away. Several neighbors had stopped by to bring her an article or some magazine that mentioned the story—she'd sent everyone home without even bothering to look. Every reminder just made her more angry. She had determined to ignore it as much as possible.

After wiping her hands on a dishrag, she took a deep breath and went to the door. She steeled herself for a confrontation in case it was indeed a press representative that had ignored the trespassing signs.

When she opened the door, she froze.

"Hello, Delilah. I'm Trisha Pompiskoloski," the blonde said. "I took a chance and ignored the sign. Can I come in and talk to you for a moment?"

Twenty minutes later Delilah stared at the small tape player that had just finished playing back the conversation Trisha had had with Sam the day before. Next to the tape player was a box of fourteen videos, labeled by their date—dates that coincided with Sam's stay. Trisha claimed they were the original tapes. She showed Delilah the signed contracts from Cody. But it was still hard to swallow Her conversation with Leif just two days ago seemed to shout at her.

"You say that Sam didn't know about this recording," Delilah said. "How do I know that's true and not just another Hollywood game?"

"You don't," Trisha said bluntly. "And I have no way to prove it other than giving you my word."

Delilah considered that for a few moments. "I don't have a lot of faith in the word of Hollywood types," she said honestly. "I have no reason to believe you."

"You're absolutely right," Trish said with a nod. "But you do have these tapes and the contracts. That should say something."

It did, but Delilah was still hesitant. She looked at Trisha. "What's in this for you?" She had learned enough to know that no one did something like this for no reason.

"Actually, I was hoping you'd do me a favor . . . two in fact."

"I knew it," Delilah said, leaning back and folding her arms across her chest.

"Now, don't get upset," Trisha said. "The tapes are yours regardless of what you decide. But if you're willing to consider it, I would like you to go to the Oscars with Sam."

Delilah took a breath.

"I know you don't want to, and I understand why. But

something happened to Sam out here. He grew up and sees the world differently. He's going to win that award tomorrow night, and he deserves to accept it in person."

"I asked what was in it for you, not him."

Trisha hedged for just a moment. "I want to interview you."

"Mrs. Pom-pis—co—p—"

"Just call me Trisha," she broke in.

"Okay . . . Trisha. I have been doing everything in my power to avoid the press. The last thing I want to do is an interview. In another week this will have all gone away. I don't want to start it up again."

"I figured you would say that, so I brought one last thing to try and sway you. Of course you can still say no, and I will not force your hand. But you need to realize what you've done to this country over the last week. It's really quite phenomenal. Surely you've seen the hype?"

"We have no TV, my phone has been off the hook, and you saw the sign on the gate. I've been shut up in my house for six days. Several neighbors have brought over articles, but I haven't even bothered to read them. That should explain to you why I'm not your girl. I hate this stuff, I just want it to go away."

Trisha reached into her bag and removed a manila envelope. She handed it to Delilah, who regarded it with confusion. "Open it," Trisha said.

Delilah lifted the flap and extracted what looked like a magazine cover, without any pages inside. The back of the cover was facing her with an advertisement.

She flipped it over to see the front. On the cover was a throng of young girls wearing T-shirts that said "I am Delilah." In bright red letters across the front of the cover it read, "Are modest girls the hottest girls?"

Delilah's mouth fell open and she looked up at Trisha. "What is this?"

"It's a mock up of the cover for next week's *People Magazine*. You've started a revolution."

"Me?"

"Do you remember a certain conversation you had with

Sam about the Versace dress?"

Delilah thought back. "Yes," she finally answered when she had recalled the conversation.

"Well, it was in the batch of clips that Cody leaked to the presses. It didn't run at first because there were so many other clips that made Sam look like a moron. But after your press conference, this one hit the airwaves. It has created a national following. There's a call for girls to dress like ladies, a reclamation of virtue and modesty. And you, my dear girl, are the ringleader."

"But . . . I didn't even know about it."

"Which is why I would love to do a story on you. What do you say?"

Delilah looked at her hands in her lap. After nearly a minute of reflection she lifted her head. "Honestly, Trisha, I've had my fill of cameras and press. I'm flattered that so many girls would want to adopt some of my standards, but I really just want to live my normal life again."

Trisha nodded. "That's another thing that makes you so interesting. I'll tell you what—if you give me this interview, I'll do everything I can to call off the dogs."

"Can you do that?"

"Are you kidding? I'm Trisha P."

"Hmm," Delilah said. "I'll have to think about it."

"Will you go to the Oscars?"

Delilah let out a long breath and Leif's words rang in her mind. *How many people get the opportunity to step into another world?* She mentally reviewed the tape Trisha had brought—it did sound sincere. She looked at her hands and thought of all the things Sam had gone through here on the farm. If he didn't leak the tapes, then he was as much a victim as she was—more, perhaps, since the clips were so horrid. She looked up and met Trisha's hopeful gaze. "I'll do it," she said.

Trisha broke into a wide grin.

"I'll wear my own dress," Delilah continued.

"Uh, I have a few you could choose from waiting in LA— would you consider—"

"No," Delilah broke in. "You said you wanted to interview *me*. This is who I am. I want to wear this dress . . . but it's not quite done. Is there any way we could have a seamstress finish it in time?"

"This is Hollywood, my dear. We can do anything."

⭐ Chapter Twelve ⭐

The next morning, Rhett drove Delilah and the nearly finished dress to the small airport in Cedar City. At ten A.M. she
was escorted to the plane. Trisha had stayed the night in Cedar
City—renting out an entire bed and breakfast for her crew—
and waited until this morning to take Delilah to California
with her. Delilah needed the time to review the tapes and get
packed. Delilah put her garment bag and suitcase down and sat
in a leather recliner, willing her heart to stop pounding. She'd
lain awake most of the night trying to decide if this was the
right choice. *Too late now,* she realized.

"Is that your dress?" Trisha asked once they were in the air,
indicating the dress bag.

Delilah nodded.

"May I see it?"

Delilah nodded again and took it out. Trisha rubbed the red
fabric between her fingers and looked at it long and hard. "It's
very nice—but are you sure you wouldn't like to at least look
at the dresses I had delivered?"

Delilah let out a breath. "I'm wearing this dress. It reflects
who I am, and I'm not going to negotiate. I feel like I've made
plenty of concessions already. It's not open for discussion."

Trisha was silent. "You really are an unusual girl, aren't
you?"

"Depends on where you're from."

Trisha laughed. "Will you let me have someone help you
with the hair and makeup?"

"As long as they don't make me look like Tami Faye."

"Oh, no, it will be very classy."

"Then I'd love the help."

★★★

Sam awoke on Oscar Sunday and stared at the blinds covering his windows. He looked at the alarm clock—8:37. He considered staying in bed all day, but what good would that do? After Trisha had left Thursday afternoon, Sam had called around and found a new assistant. Trisha's visit had sparked in him a desire to start living again, and he knew he needed an assistant to help him fix things. But it would be different than it had been before. Ricky Andres had been an assistant for Katie Couric and came highly recommended. He wasn't Cody, but that was probably a good thing.

Ricky had the coffee brewing and a bagel waiting to be toasted. "Can I get you anything else?" Ricky asked when Sam got down stairs.

"I'm good," Sam said. "In fact, why don't you take the day off."

"Off?"

"Yeah, you know—go do your own stuff, meet people." *Get a life!* he added in is mind. It was surprising, now that he'd had such a wake-up call, that it hadn't bothered him to have Cody around as much as he had. He'd been at Sam's beck and call for over a year. Not that it didn't have its perks for Sam. But he knew now that there was more to life than getting his every whim fulfilled. He hadn't forgiven Cody for what he'd done, but he planned to learn from this experience. The first step was not to get so dependant on his new assistant.

Ricky looked confused. "Really?"

"Absolutely," Sam said. "I'd like to spend the day alone, if you don't mind."

"Well, sure," Ricky finally said.

Once Ricky was gone, Sam went out to his new woodshop. He'd had Ricky buy a few different saws and a pile of wood. On the Internet he'd downloaded the plans for a magazine rack and was glad that during the last few days on the farm Rhett had given him a good education on tool safety. Life would be a real bummer if he cut off his hand trying to build a magazine rack. His new hobby wasn't going all that well, but he liked the smell of the wood and at least it felt like he was accomplishing something. He was sure his persistence would pay off eventually. As he measured and cut, he couldn't help wondering what Delilah was doing. Every time he thought of her and her family, he felt like he had a rock in his stomach. He hated being powerless to fix things. Hopefully the tapes Trisha was going to send them would help them find forgiveness for what he'd done to their lives.

After a couple of hours, and still not being able to cut the sides of the magazine rack quite right, he went inside and decided to take a shower. He still had a few scripts he was supposed to review, but he wasn't in the mood. Self-introspection was highly overrated.

His phone rang, and he wavered about answering it—there were only two people that knew the new number: Ricky and Trisha P.

"Hello?"

"Sam it's Trisha—I've been trying to get a hold of you all morning."

"I've been outside . . . working," he said, knowing it sounded ridiculous. She wouldn't believe that for a second. "What can I do for you?"

"Remember when I said you owed me one?"

"Yes," he said slowly.

"Well, I want to collect. I want you to go to the Oscars tonight."

"Trisha, I've already made up my mind," he said. "The last thing I need tonight is a thousand microphones shoved in my face while they ask me about killing all those chickens. I'd rather stay home. Can't I just come and paint your house or shovel manure for you instead?"

"Sam," she said with sincerity. "Please reconsider—you need to go. You need to make a stand, show that you can still hold your head up."

"*Can* I still hold my head up?"

"Sam, I'm the first one to admit that the attention you've

received lately has been . . . less than flattering. But you are still Sam Hendricks, and you're going to win tonight. You really need to go."

Sam wavered a little, and it took another five minutes for her to convince him.

"Why does this matter to you so much?" Sam finally asked.

"Because despite your faults, you're a good man, and you don't deserve what's happened. Besides, you owe me that favor for sending those tapes to Delilah. Please go."

"Uhhhhhhh . . . "

"I'll send my car around for you at six—be ready."

"I have my own car," he said, but there was simply a click on the line. If it had been anyone other than Trisha P, he'd have told them to jump in a lake—but he did owe her a favor . . . and it *was* the Oscars, after all.

At a few minutes to six, Trisha's driver used the intercom system to request entrance. Sam pushed the button that would open the gates. There was a knock at the door just as he was doing up the top button of his Hugo Boss Tuxedo. The Prada shoes he had on clicked across the marble entryway as he walked to the door. He was still in the process of fastening his monogrammed cufflinks as he opened the door, expecting to see Trisha's driver.

His mouth fell open. Delilah was standing on the doorstep.

"Hi Sam," she said. She was dressed in the red floor-length gown he'd seen Mary working on. It wasn't a designer gown, but it was a lot better than the prom dress, and it fit her like a glove. The color of the fabric made her skin glow. Her makeup was perfect, and her thick blonde hair was pulled up in a style that could only have been achieved by a professional. At that moment Sam was hard pressed to recollect a single woman in his memory that looked as beautiful as Delilah did right now.

It was several seconds before the shock wore off enough for him to speak. "What . . . what are you doing here?"

She shrugged. "I changed my mind."

There were another few moments of delay. "Just like that?"

Delilah shrugged. "Not really—Leif and Trisha P helped."

"Trisha?"

"She brought me the tapes yesterday—and a recording of a certain conversation the two of you had here in your house. You really should be careful about your friends. Anyway, it tipped the scales."

Sam was thoughtful for several seconds. "I . . . I can't believe you're here."

"Well," she said, cocking her head to the side. "It *is* the Oscars."

They talked all the way to The Kodak Theatre in Hollywood. When they took their place in the line of limos waiting to be announced on the red carpet, Delilah got quiet.

"You're going to do great," Sam said with a smile. He still couldn't believe she was here. His heart had wings.

Delilah looked down at herself and smoothed the fabric across her thighs. "Maybe you were right about the dress."

"Of course I was right about the dress."

She gave him a dirty look across the leather seats. "You're not helping."

He laughed. "I'm kidding. You look beautiful." He wished he dared tell her just how beautiful she looked, but he feared it would put the wrong feeling on the night, and he didn't want to put her off. But she was striking, and it was hard not to tell her so—or better yet, show her so.

"Really?"

"What," he said, putting his hand on his chest for dramatic impression and ignoring his growing attraction. "Delilah is out of her comfort zone? Would you like me to have the driver take us by the petting zoo or something—maybe they'll let you milk a goat really quick."

"Very funny," she said dryly. Then she looked out the window again. There were only two cars ahead of them now. She started fidgeting, and Sam placed his hand over hers. She looked up and met his eyes.

"You put up with having me in your house for two whole weeks. You milked a hundred cows twice a day and cleaned up dead chickens. This will not be that bad."

"They're going to make fun of my dress," she said with a vulnerability Sam had never seen in her. " I know they will."

"Is what people think of you the only thing that matters?" he mimicked. "Is it all about playing some part for you?"

Delilah threw up her hands and couldn't help but smile. "I've created a monster."

"But I'm a better monster because of you," he said with a wink.

She shook her head and looked out the window with growing apprehension as the car moved forward one last time. "It's our turn, isn't it?"

Sam moved toward the door and reached out his hand. "You're going to knock them dead."

She placed her hand in his, and he gently closed his fingers around her own. "Let's just hope that I'm better at living in your world than you were at living in mine," she said.

As soon as she finished talking, the door opened. He pulled her with him as he stepped out of the car. For an instant the crowd seemed quiet. But as soon as she got out of the car and stood up straight, the hordes of people erupted. Flashbulbs exploded in her face, and she tightened her grip on Sam's hand. He pulled her close and whispered in her ear, "Smile."

She smiled.

Someone called her name, and she turned to see more brilliant flashes. Still smiling, she leaned toward Sam and said through her teeth, "They're going to blind me."

Sam laughed and put one arm around her shoulder. "It will only last a day or two."

Suddenly, a microphone was thrust into Delilah's face. "Delilah, what made you change your mind about coming tonight?"

"Uh." She froze and didn't know what to say. Sam nudged her with his elbow, and her brain started moving again. "I guess you could say it was . . . mercy."

The crowd roared. Sam shook his head with a smile.

"A mercy date," the interviewer repeated. "Who'd have thought Sam Hendricks would ever need one of those?"

Delilah felt herself relaxing. These were just people. Maybe they weren't the people she was used to interacting with, but they were people all the same. Her confidence came back like a boomerang, and she stood up straighter. "Everyone deserves a second chance. Sam gave me his word, and I came to realize that he didn't break it after all."

Someone else yelled out a question. "Who's dress are you wearing?"

She felt Sam cringe next to her, but she didn't skip a beat. "This is a Mary Glenshaw original."

There was a collective pause. "Your mother?" someone asked.

"Yep," she said with a big smile. "She's very talented, and frankly it's impossible to find a dress in the store that doesn't show too much—if you know what I mean."

For the next thirty minutes she and Sam posed for what seemed like a thousand photographs. More questions were asked about her dress and her change of heart. She and Sam answered them with friendly bantering answers. He didn't leave her side, and she was eternally grateful for that. At one point a photographer asked for a photo of the two of them sharing a kiss. Delilah shook her head "no" but Sam had another idea. He took two steps back and lifted Delilah's right hand. He bowed deeply at the waist, put one arm behind his back, and kissed her hand. Delilah laughed, and the flashbulbs looked like atomic bombs going off.

It was all a whirl of cameras and microphones, interspersed with introductions to the who's who of the movie marquees. She met Sandra Bullock and Jack Nicholson, as well as Julia Roberts and her all-time favorite actor, Sean Connery. After what seemed like mere moments—but was actually nearly an hour—she and Sam found their seats.

The big moment finally arrived when the presenters announced that the next award was for best actor. She leaned over and took Sam's hand, squeezing it with anticipation. "And the nominees are . . . Johnny Depp . . . Leonardo DiCaprio . . . Ben Affleck . . . Sam Hendricks . . . and Benjamin Bratt . . . and the winner is . . ." Delilah held her breath, and Sam squeezed her hand tighter.

"Sam Hendricks!" The room exploded, and Sam and Delilah looked at one another in shock. In the next second they were on their feet. She hugged him tightly and stayed on her feet clapping and jumping until he got up to the podium.

He cleared his throat before he began his speech. "Honestly, after all that's happened over the last week I didn't expect to be standing here. I . . . I'm truly honored." His voice was sincere, and Delilah sat back down while listening intently. "Until about two o'clock this afternoon I wasn't planning to be here tonight, and it wasn't until this evening that I realized Delilah was coming with me." Whispers of surprise swept through the audience, and his gaze settled on Delilah for just a moment before he scanned the crowd again.

"I would like to thank all those that worked so hard on the film. We had an amazing cast, and I wouldn't be here without them. I wish to offer public apologies to my fans for not being the man I should have been at this time in my life. I'm working on it."

A small laugh moved like a wave through the crowd. "But mostly, I'd like to thank the Glenshaw family. Putting up with me was hard enough. Putting up with everything that followed has been more than they deserve. I will always treasure the time I spent in their home, although I'll never look at a glass of milk quite the same." Another laugh. "And last, but certainly not least, I would like to thank Delilah for being a woman of integrity and showing me a world I honestly didn't know existed. I would like to wish her and Leif Thompson every happiness, and I want her to know that I plan to take her advice and become the kind of man that a woman such as herself would one day want to spend her life with." He paused and turned his eyes to the audience again. "Thank you to the Academy, I am truly honored." He walked away, and Delilah gave him a standing ovation.

✮ Chapter Thirteen ✮

After the awards they made their way back to the limo, enduring more photographs along the way. Once inside Sam let out a whoop of joy. "I really can't believe I won!" he yelled with the enthusiasm of a quarterback after making the winning touchdown.

"I'm sure you earned it," she said with a smile. It was amazing to be a part of something this big.

Sam leaned against the back of the seat and undid the top button of his shirt. "Do you ever think you'll watch one of my movies?"

"Not if they're all rated R," she said. "Why don't you use your talent to do something good . . . something funny and wholesome. Something I could watch with my parents and my kids?"

"Well, maybe I will," Sam said with a grin. "If I do, will you come to the premiere with me?"

"I'll be a married woman by then—so no, I won't. But Leif and I will watch it when it comes out in Cedar City. I'll write and tell you what I think."

"It's a deal, but don't tell me what you think. I'm not sure I could take it."

She laughed and asked what was next.

"Well, I was invited to go to some parties—do you want to do that?"

"Umm, not really," she admitted. "But I will if you want me to."

Sam gave her a sideways look. "Would you really?"

"Sure," she said with obvious hesitation. "This is my night in your world. I'll do whatever you want—within reason."

And it was set. They went to the party at Sardi's restaurant, and Delilah, although not having the time of her life, had a very good time. She was glad she was a good dancer. She was introduced to even more celebrities and had Sam take her picture with a few of her favorites. They were for her scrapbook, she said. He didn't know what she was talking about.

Around two o'clock in the morning the limo pulled out of the parking lot. Sam turned to look at Delilah. Her hair was staring to fall from her fancy hairdo, and she looked tired, but happy. It felt good to have been a part of something she enjoyed. She'd been a wonderful companion all night; kind, funny, elegant—he couldn't have choreographed a better evening. "Where are you staying?" he asked.

"At the Beverly Wilshire. The Jacuzzi tub in that room is the size of my entire bathroom at home."

"That small?"

She slugged him in the arm—none too lightly—and they both got quiet. A few minutes later the limo pulled under the elaborate Porte coche. A bellman immediately began walking toward them, and Sam realized these were his last few moments in her company.

"Thanks for coming tonight, Delilah. I had a great time."

"I'm glad I did," she said with a smile. "I had a great time, too."

Her smile was so entrancing, and he wanted to make her stay. He inched closer, and she pulled back. "Don't ruin it," she said softly. "We've already had this conversation."

He moved back and nodded. "It was worth a try."

"No, it wasn't." But she smiled, and he understood that she wasn't angry. He was glad for that.

"Will you invite me to the wedding?" he asked.

"It will be in the St. George temple. You can't come in. But I'd love to have you come to the reception, if you can come without an entourage."

"I'll be there with bells on," Sam said. They went quiet again and looked at one another for several seconds. "Leif's a lucky guy, ya know."

"Thanks, I'll tell him you said so."

"I guess you won after all."

"Won?" she asked.

"You did better in my world than I did in yours."

"But I only had to put up with your world for one day—it wasn't really a fair trade."

"Baloney," Sam said with a shake of his head. "I deserved everything I got."

"Did you just say 'baloney'?"

They both laughed and her door opened. She put one foot out of the limo before turning to face him one last time. "I'll always remember this as one of the most amazing nights of my life," she said.

Sam smiled. "So will I," he said. "But, because of you, I'm going to live my life in such a way that it's not *the* best night of my life. You showed me that there is more than this."

Delilah couldn't help but grin widely. "There is so much more," she said. "Now that you realize it, this will be just the beginning."

✭ Epilogue ✭

The picture of Sam kissing Delilah's hand showed up on magazine covers across the country. It replaced the picture of Delilah's fans on *People Magazine*, but the articles were the same. On Thursday following the Academy Awards, Delilah was featured on *One on One with Trisha P.* The opening question was what Delilah stood for and what she was about. Her answer was, "Honesty, integrity, family, and virtue."

Much of the interview consisted of Delilah explaining what that meant. She was also asked questions about Sam's visit, and she answered with humorous honesty.

After that interview, the Delilah fans across the nation increased ten fold. There was a demand for prom dresses with sleeves and backs, as well as shirts that weren't cut for cleavage. The following spring runways boasted longer skirts and higher necklines. Coincidence? Trisha didn't think so.

Ralph Lauren paid Delilah an exorbitant amount of money to use her name to launch a new clothing line that reflected her standards. The money was used to buy a parcel of land a few miles down the road from her parents. Construction began almost immediately, with Leif doing much of the work himself.

Sam accepted a role in the film *Nice Guys Finish First* a month following Oscar nominations. It would be his first PG movie, and sources were already saying it might just win him another Oscar. He was spending more time away from the camera lens these days and had recently donated a few pieces of hand-made furniture to a charity auction. The Dairy Farmers of America had complained about his anti-milk comments, so he'd made a generous donation to numerous charities that benefited their agenda and made a "Got Milk" ad that was likely the most successful advertisement the Dairy Council had ever had. It was the first time he drank milk since his stay at the

Glenshaw farm—it was refreshing.

On April tenth, Leif and Delilah were married in the St.George temple. There had been no announcements sent, for fear that the press would want to be involved. Instead, they called those they wanted in attendance the night before. Most of them were able to make it. The only cameras present were those held by family members and one photographer hired to capture the best day of their lives for Delilah's scrapbook.

That night, the parents of the bride, along with the parents of the groom, threw a party for Leif and Delilah unlike anything Big Fork had ever seen. The announcement had barely come out in that day's paper, and the entire town had been invited to come celebrate with the couple that had put their town on the map.

About halfway through the bash, a rather unobtrusive black car pulled into the overflowing parking lot. When Sam entered the hall a short time later with none other than Neil Diamond beside him, Mary nearly fainted.

The dance hall practically exploded. Before the night had ended, Mary stood in front of her home town and sang *You Don't Bring Me Flowers* with Neil and the ward pianist as accompaniment. Following her duet, she and Rhett danced as Neil sang her favorite song of all time, *Hello Again.*

The evening ended with Leif giving heartfelt thanks to everyone who had attended, before whisking his bride out the door and helping her get into the whipping-cream-and-Oreo-laden car.

Sam and Neil stayed to help clean up and Mary went home with an autographed copy of *The Jazz Singer.*

Fifty miles away, Leif opened the door to the honeymoon suite of the bed-and-breakfast where he and Delilah would spend their first night of forever together.

Leif lifted his bride over the threshold and spun her around before putting her down. Then he pulled her into his arms.

"Did you think we'd ever really get here?" he asked.

"There were moments when I wondered," she admitted.

"And now that we're here, do you have any regrets?"

"Only one."

Leif raised his eyebrows.

"I really should have stood my ground with that chicken massacre. It was all his fault, you know. And I just backed down and helped him clean it up. That's the only thing I really regret. I mean—"

Leif silenced her with a long kiss. When he finally pulled back, he put his forehead against hers. "That wasn't what I meant."

"Oh, well it's the only regret I have."

"You sure?"

"Leif," she said. "You are the kind of man that makes being a girl like me all worthwhile. I have never, for a moment, wanted anything other than what I have right now." She kissed him again. "And I never want to discuss it again—understand?"

"Yes, ma'am," he said with a laugh. Then he pulled her tightly against his chest and whispered, "Now, where were we?"

✯ About the Author ✯

In addition to four children, Breanna, Madison, Christopher, and Kylee, Josi and her husband, Lee, also raised a niece for several years, Lindsy, and therefore claim to be the proud parents of five children and grandparents of one. Josi and her family live in Willard, Utah where they enjoy the outdoors, travel, and time with their kids. Josi actively serves in her ward and loves to hear from her readers. Please feel free to contact her at Kilpack@favorites.com or www.josiskilpack.com.